Other Books

An Assortment of Poetry

Scattered Emotions

Inspired Thoughts

Acknowledgements

I would like to give a very special thank you firstly, to my friends, family, and coworkers for putting up with me these years of working on this project. A very big thank you to Becket for the referral to his friend, Todd for editing. A thank you to Todd Barselow for putting up with me during the editing process. And most importantly, to my famdom family. Without them, the editing would have never even happened. You showed me love and support throughout this whole ride. You never gave up on me. You reminded me I was not alone and to always keep fighting through to get my impala done. There are so many of you, that I wouldn't possibly know who to begin with! You all know who you are, and I love you all. So here she is! Done and ready for you all to read and I hope enjoy and cherish as well. Much love and many blessings to each and every one of you.

Their Hope Within

The Flames

By Sky Boivin

We were just a quiet New England family. I couldn't even tell you exactly when the chaos all came about. All I know is that I lost my sisters and now I must move away from this village I have called home all my life and start fresh. There is no staying here. Not now. The wagon is packed and waiting for me upon the far hillside as I watch my last sister go. Almost the last of my family. The last of my family is standing on the landing below, watching the spectacle. She's standing close for a front row view.

But, that one is dead to me now. I must flee from this place before she sets her sights on me next or the child standing behind me. I must watch over and protect Samie on my own now. I must teach her to be safe; safer than we were so that what happened to our family won't be repeated.

* * *   Some months ago   * * *

It was just another regular morning. Cloe and I were outside early, tending to the garden. We were collecting what foods we could for breakfast before the birds got to them and left us nothing. Just another normal morning, or so we thought. We saw a wagon coming up from the road towards the cottage.

"Is that Nicloas's wagon?" I asked, pointing to the road.

"It appears to be," Cloe answered. She tried to hide a smile. We watched the wagon drive up. There was a female in the seat next to him.

'Who is that seated next to him?' I thought to Cloe curiously. We both wondered.

Sometimes we didn't have to open our mouths to speak. We could communicate with our thoughts. No one else seemed to be able to do this in the village but our family. So we kept it to ourselves. Or so we thought.

As the wagon came closer, we noticed that it was our cousin, Tabitha. She was sitting smugly next to Nicolas. She had such a stern look on her face to try and hide the smugness within. She had some new cruel plan going on in her head. I just knew it. She never looked like that unless she was brewing up trouble for someone.

The wagon stopped in front of our small cottage, and Nicolas jumped down from the seat. His round rimmed black hat flopped as he did so. He went around to help Tabitha out of the wagon. He tilted his hat.

"Ladies," he said.

"Nicolas," Cloe replied back. They paused for a moment and looked at each other.

"What's wrong?" I blurted out.

Cloe shot me a look. *'Shhhh!'* she yelled in my head. I looked at my feet. I could not help it. Straight to the point is the way I preferred things. No wasting time beating around the bush.

Of course Tabitha gave a sly smirk as Nicolas hoisted her off of the wagon. "Hello cousins. Is it not a lovely day out today?"

That smirk had always made me uncomfortable when we were growing up. Almost as though you could *hear* the gears inside her brain running full speed for whatever god-forsaken plan she was cooking up to get someone, anyone into trouble. Just so she could get whatever she wanted.

"Good day, Tabitha. What brings you out so early this quiet morning? Don't you need your beauty sleep?" Emy spoke from the doorway of the cottage. Her mouse brown hair was braided to one side under her cap.

Tabitha froze mid-step. It was clear she was afraid of Emy. She'd never dared cross her unawares since we were kids. She learnt that one real quick. They were secretly sworn enemies. We as a family were the only ones who knew why it was so. Ever since that day by the river, Tabitha had always tried what she could to be rid of Emy for good. I think her pride was hurt more than anything after what had actually happened. The green-eyed monster of jealousy can be real mean...

But, I digress.

"May we talk inside, Madam?" Nicolas addressed Emy.

"Yes, this way." She led them into the dirt floor kitchen. The fire was already roaring and the biscuits were warming on the side oven. The smell was enough to make one hungry. Emy pointed to a pair of chairs for Nicolas and Tabitha to be seated. Cloe and I looked at each other as we silently debated if we should sit in on the conversation or not.

'Maybe we should let them be. If we need be knowing about it, Emy will tell us later,' Cloe thought to me. I nodded and we turned to make way for the door.

"This actually concerns all of you," Nicolas said.

Emy nodded for us to remain as well. We sat opposite Tabitha and Nicolas. Emy sat at the head of the table. While her husband, Aaron, was away at sea, she had become head of the household and everyone and everything went through her.

Nicolas sighed. He was extremely nervous about what he had to say. It couldn't be good news, judging by the look on his face.

'*My God, has something happened to Aaron's ship? Are they all okay?*' My mind raced with frantic, doomsday thoughts.

'*Hush, child. Let him speak before you race those thoughts into the air,*' Emy poked in.

I lowered eyes to the table as though scolded. I knew she was right. I was getting ahead of myself. But I never really thought it could be anything else, that anything could be worse than losing a family member at sea.

"There have been rumors around the village." Nicolas paused. He glanced around the room. "Rumors that are not so good. They are about your family. Namely about Cloe." He briefly caught Cloe's eyes with his then they shot away from her.

Emy just sat there and nodded as though she already knew. Probably because she did. Did she know what Nicolas was going to say? She'd always had that intuitiveness about her. She drove us nuts with it sometimes. But we each had a different level of that in our own way.

"Oh get on with it man!" Tabitha burst into what Nicolas was trying to say. "What kind of a man are you?" Her voice resonated along the walls of the even more suffocating kitchen. "They are saying that Cloe is a witch, that she's a child of the Devil. They swear she's been cursing crops on the next farm over!"

Witch.

The word reverberated in my head. It seemed to echo into the depths of my mind for eternity. Witch? Cloe? Not in the sense that they think of witch. She could chat up with the birds to help carry seeds for planting. And she could get the bees to play with the flowers sooner to help them seed faster. She used that ability to help the gardens grow and prosper. But she would *never* harm another farm. If anything, she would send the bees over to help them.

No. This couldn't be right. They had it all wrong. Maybe a disease plowed through their crop. Maybe they did something different from what they normally did and it backfired.

Anything but this.

I looked at Tabitha. She sat there smugly. She was so proud of herself over this.

'You bastard', I reeled in my head. *'This is your doing. I know it. You want something. And by God I will find out what it is real soon. You will be stopped.'* I glared at Tabitha. Her eyes snapped over to me as though I had just slapped her from across the table. The smile disappeared from her face. I knew she felt the cold chill that was sent her way by my glare.

Tabitha's eyes went away from me and she shivered. "I think there is a draft in here," she said to Nicolas shyly.

Nicolas ignored her. I think he was still dumbfounded by her taking over the conversation.

"They will like to see Cloe as soon as possible. Do not try and hide her or let her escape for safety. It will look bad on all of you. Especially with Aaron and the others still at sea. You can plead for a waiting period until they have returned from their trip so that they can help with her trial. But there is no promise they will grant even that much. If you will excuse me, I will leave you to your thoughts on this matter. They will call upon Cloe when they are ready for her." Nicolas stood up from the table.

Emy grabbed Nicolas's arm. "Thank you for the heads-up on this. You are a good man, Nicolas. Bless you," she said to him. Nicolas nodded and made his way to the door.

"I shall be out in one moment, Nicolas," Tabitha said without looking behind her. She had her own business to tend to now and she did not need Nicolas to hear what she had to say to us. When the door closed behind Nicolas, Tabitha started, "Well, this is quite the pickle you have gotten us into, Cloe. Now is it not?"

Cloe just sat there as if frozen by Medusa's gaze. I wondered if she was still breathing. I could feel the fiery anger building up within me. Tabitha had no place to say such a thing.

"Her? Her! What in the blazes of Hell are you talking about, Tabitha? Do you even *hear* yourself? You know bloody well Cloe would have never harmed anything! Let alone someone else's *farm*! What have *you* done to this family? What are you after, Tabitha? Maybe we should have let you die that day by the river instead of trying to save your sorry ass because of your stupidity!" I finally screamed. Tears raged down my face. I threw my hands up in the air in exasperation. The walls echoed with my voice. I threw myself down upon the dirt floor, sobbing heavily.

Emy rose slowly from the table. Calm and collected, she walked towards Tabitha. She stood facing her for what seemed like forever. I watched silently to see what may happen. I could see the nervousness in Tabitha's eyes.

"I think it is best if you never step foot inside our home again, cousin. You are no longer welcome here. After the situation you have bestowed upon this roof, you are no longer our kin," Emy whispered upon the air of the silent kitchen. The room seemed frozen. Even the roaring fire seemed to be lost in time.

Tabitha stood silent a while longer, contemplating what to say. "So be it, cousin. I shall see you at the trials then." With that, she flew out of the cottage and to Nicolas in the awaiting wagon.

The three of us sat there in the kitchen, wondering what was going to happen next. The whole cottage was silent except for the crackle of the fire that seemed to have come back to life again.

The next few months flew by in a blur. They came and "examined" Cloe. They said she had "the Devil's Mark." What mark it was they wouldn't say. They feared that we might try to hide it or have it removed somehow. They denied our request to wait for Aaron's ship to return home so that some of the other family members could be present. They reasoned that since there was no way to know how much longer they would be at sea or if they would even return at all, they could not possibly wait. The council felt that we might try to sneak her aboard the ship and have it set sail during the night.

Next thing we knew, the words *guilty of witchcraft* rang out through the stuffy town hall. The hall was filled with both cheers and murmurs. I wanted to scream out at all of them. Cloe kept looking straight towards the back of the hall. Who could she possibly be looking at? She always looked towards the back. Never at anyone or anything else. There was such a sea of villagers and travelers who came just to see the trial of the witch that they all blurred together.

Before we knew it, it was the morning of the burning. The council did grant us a few moments alone with our sister so we could say our goodbyes. She had been kept in a filthy cell where rats could come up and eat at your body. Poor Cloe was covered in dust and dirt. Her raven hair was all disheveled and knotted. We just sat there in silence holding each other's hands, waiting. Waiting for the time for them to take Cloe to her fate. To her death.

A wrongful death.

We could hear the men outside tossing more logs onto the area where the burning was to take place. A knock on the cell door broke our silence. We all looked up, knowing the inevitable time had come.

Nicolas popped his head in. "It is time for you two to leave now. I see them starting to get ready to come over. I have let you stay longer than they'd have liked," he whispered.

Emy and I got up slowly. We didn't want to leave Cloe alone. We also didn't want more trouble than there already was. We ducked out of the small cell and into the forest line so no one else would see us leaving. We went to a quiet and safe spot away from all of the commotion so we could speak without anyone listening in.

"We must do something about Tabitha. She is up to no good. This is just the beginning of her plan."

"It's not her fault. She has been brainwashed," Emy said quietly.

I looked at her, puzzled. "Brainwashed? By who? Who could have come up with THIS?" I stopped in my tracks. I was stunned that Emy would choose now, this moment, to start defending Tabitha. After all these years.

"I saw her speaking with the new brother of the church. I've sent letters to Brother Thompson in England about him. He has been moved around from church to church, a lot. Each village he goes to seems to have burnings once he gets there. They have all been quiet little villages like ours. Until he shows up." The forest fell silent. We looked around to make sure no one else was around.

"He has been heading up witch burnings left and right. From what I received in letters about him, he finds one main female to "help" him pin things on everyone else until she is the only one left. Then he makes the village turn against her. To somehow say that it must have been her all along. That she headed it all up. That she is the witch. That the others were serving her, and that she serves HIM. Once she has been burned, the church conveniently moves him along to another village to "continue" his work."

I stood frozen, a chill crawling along my spine. I couldn't believe my ears. Had Emy just said all this, or did I imagine it? This just had to be a bad dream. The church couldn't possibly be behind this... No. It couldn't be. Maybe they just didn't realize what was going on. That must be it.

"Should we tell someone? What should we do? I, I..." I stammered.

"WE will say nothing. You will act shocked, just like you are right now. I will get more information on this bastard who claims to be doing God's work. I will expose him for what he is. I will end his reign here. And justify Cloe and all the other innocents he has already taken from this world."

Emy's eyes glowed brightly in the shadows. She burned with energy and it built up fast within her. She wanted to strike this man down right where he stood. I could see that in her eyes. But I knew she was also building up the self-control further below that to *not* do so. At least not today of all days. That would make it ten times worse for all of us. I understood that now. She taught me that one. Keep quiet and keep to yourself. Don't let others know what you can do or what you behold. Trouble will be a foot if you do otherwise.

Then it hit me. Her. She'd only said *her*. What in the world could she possibly be thinking of doing, and why was I not included? Could she be fated the same as Cloe if she opens her mouth and exposes this Devil within the church? This monstrous demon who is going on a church funded killing spree that they may not even realize is being done?

She looked deep into my eyes. "I will expose that demon even if it kills me, which it may."

That's what I was afraid of. Damn it all to Hell! Even now, just to protect everyone else around her, Emy would go to any length to save them even if it meant the end her own life. Sounds extreme, but that's true, unconditional love for you. No matter what came up in life, she was ready for the fight. She would go down fighting. I knew, with the look in her eyes right then and there, she had sealed her fate. She would expose this demon alright. But she'd be burned for witchcraft in the process.

I knew it. She knew it. That's why she wants me to stay out of the way. Or to at least *act* like I don't know what's going on. Act shocked and surprised when the accusation is finally made public. But how would we do that?

I shook my head. "No, not alone you're not. I won't let you. I can play dumb when I need to. But we are in this together. Sisters stick together. Through thick and thin, no matter what."

I tried to stand my ground even though I knew she would win somehow. She always knew how to get her way, especially in a matter as deadly as this. But, I had to at least try. To show I would go down fighting for her and others, too. For some reason I felt I had to show her that much.

"We'll see what plays out. You may need to play a small, *very small* role." She winked at me and smirked.

Ah shit, I knew that smirk. I could only imagine what she had up her sleeve on that note. I smirked back at her and shook my head. At least she would let me help her with this plan of hers. Small role was better than no role at all.

"It should be just about time for them to do this blasted thing of theirs. We should get going." Emy hugged me and grabbed my hand. "Let's go or they will start talking about how her own sisters were not there." She winked at me and we ran down the path to await our sister's doom.

The villagers were already coming out to the common area to watch "the witch" burn. They had the logs piled up high. I saw Cloe tied by her hands in a far corner being led by Nicolas closer to the burning spot. It looked almost as though they had been speaking to each other quietly until they got closer. Then they seemed to stop. Surely we didn't need Nicolas falling prey to these witch hunts, too.

As they approached, someone yelled from the crowd, "Die, witch!"

"Burn in Hell you vile woman!" yelled another.

These were people we had known all of our lives. In the blink of an eye, they had turned against Cloe because someone called her a witch. Why was this so? All it took was one person to point a finger and yell witch for something that would have happened naturally anyways. She couldn't control some disease that took over that farmer's crop any more than the next person.

Such a mad stupidity amongst them all. Someone threw a rotten apple at her. She dodged it ever so slightly. But others had the same idea and she could not stop those. There were just too many to duck out of the way of.

Emy and I stayed towards the back of the crowd so we were out of the vision of wandering eyes who might want to try and point fingers at us next. Simply because we were her sisters.

They led her to the pile of awaiting logs. They looked hungry for the fire to be coming soon. As they tied her to the one large log standing upright in the center of the pile, Father Orthus Mathias started to address the crowd and Cloe.

"Cloe, you have been found guilty of witchcraft and of being one of the Devil's mistresses. You have been sentenced to death by burning to cleanse and purify your soul. Do you have any last words, witch?"

Cloe took a deep breath in. She lifted her head up to the villagers. She found us on the tree line edge. She addressed us in silence. *'I love you both. Be brave. It will all be okay soon.'* Other than that, she remained silent.

"So be it," he said. Prayers were said to help cleanse her soul so it would see the "right" path. Two men from the village took torches that stood nearby and touched them to the logs. They lit up like a hungry vulture finding fresh carcass in the desert. The fire crackled and roared loudly as it came to life.

I wanted to help. I wanted to make it stop. She was innocent of any wrong! Damn them all to Hell! The anger built up deep within me.

"No!" I cried. I started to run but Emy grabbed my arm and held me back.

"We can't go to her, my dear," she whispered.

"We must stop this." I turned towards her. My eyes grew wide with the longing to help. I could hear Cloe's silent screams of pain within my head. She remained silent on the pole. I looked at Emy. "You have the power to stop this! We can help her. We can all be together and leave this place! Why won't you help her?" Tears streamed down my face.

"Because if I do, we are all dead. They will never stop looking for us. I cannot do anything or they will never be stopped," she whispered in my ear. I stared at her for a moment. I was hurt and angry. But, I also knew she was right.

I sunk to the ground, sobbing for Cloe's pain. The fire consumed her. Her raven black hair flew up as the flames rose higher up her body. All the while, Orthus scanned the crowd for any new victims to burn next. Emy had secretly hoped she had hidden us enough in the tree line that we would not be seen by his demon eyes.

Emy held me. We sat upon the ground for what seemed like forever, sobbing quietly while Cloe's silent screams echoed within our heads. Finally, the screams came to an end. We knew at that point she was gone from us. Relief for her pain to be ended washed over me. But, grief for losing her also came over me. We slowly lifted our heads.

In front of our tear-stained faces, we only saw our sister's lifeless body lying upon the charred black logs of a dying fire. Most of the villagers had gone home or gone about the rest of their day. How they could continue about as though nothing had happened was beyond me. They should all be in the church of our Lord and praying for forgiveness for killing a girl.

The smell of the fire and burnt flesh was still upon the air. It pierced my nose. We just sat there in the silence, listening to our surroundings. Taking in the scene that lay before us. Cloe's aura was gone from her. She was gone from us. Her soul was back to the Earth. Yet, her body remained behind. Now it was time for us to return what remained of her physically to the Earth as well. When the darkness finally came, we got up together. We walked slowly towards the horrible scene that lay before us.

"Are we bringing her home?" I whispered in the silent darkness. Not even the crickets sang their songs tonight.

"Somehow," Emy said with a nod.

"Will this cloth help?" Nicolas stood up from his seat upon the ground. He had waited for us to come back to claim our sister. He held out a large white cloth. It was surely large enough to wrap her and bring her home in. We would have to bury her at home. Because of the crimes she was found guilty of for, the church would never allow her internment within their burial ground.

We laid the cloth on the ground. Nicolas gently lifted Cloe's lifeless body off of the charred logs. The embers still glowed in some spots. He was not afraid to pick her up off of them. It was almost as though he had no feeling left in his body to be harmed anymore.

He placed her within the cloth and wrapped her in it lovingly. Before he enclosed her head, he kissed her lips and whispered something in her ear. Did Nicolas love Cloe? All these years and I never noticed that? That would at least explain why he helped us. And why he offered to watch guard over her when no one else would. She was in her protector's care even though she was sentenced to death.

He lifted her up and carried her to the wagon bed so we may bring her home.

"I shall follow behind you back to your homestead. I will help you bury her," Nicolas spoke quietly as he hoisted us up to the seat of the wagon.

"You don't have to. You may find more trouble for yourself if you do," Emy started.

"I have to. I—loved her." He put his head towards the ground and looked at his feet so we would not see his tears.

I looked at Emy. *'Did he just say that? Did I hear him correctly?'*

Emy nodded back. *'I heard it, too.'*

I reached my arm out to Nicolas. "Thank you, my brother," was all I could think to say.

He lifted his head. Tears had welled up in his eyes. His heart was broken. He had watched the love of his life burn that day, and there was absolutely nothing he could have done to have stopped it. My heart went out to him. My eyes welled up for him as well. I nodded to him. I risked the thought speech to him. *'Let us be going now before they see us,'* I tried to tell him. He looked at me to make sure he heard it right.

"Yes, yes. Let us be going before anyone sees us take her away," he agreed.

Back at the cottage, we pulled up silently. The stars shone bright and the moon was full. Nicolas pulled up alongside of us. He helped us off of the wagon. Then he went to go carry Cloe.

"She had said something to me this morning about wishing to see the old willow one more time," Nicolas said in the silence. It felt so long since either of us had spoken that it jolted me from my thoughts.

"Then that is where we shall bury her. Her favorite spot," Emy agreed. "Sounds befitting. She always loved that tree. A serene spot for a serene soul."

So we carried her body to the old willow. The moonlight shone lightly through the long flowing branches. There was one large section of moonlight that had caught my eye.

"There." I pointed. A lone wolf stood near the patch of light. The wolf was covered in dirt. He lifted his head lower to the ground in greeting. I walked closer to him.

"Good evening, old friend," I addressed the wolf. As I came closer, I noticed a long hole that he had dug. It was fresh. "Have you been waiting long for us? Looks like you have been busy tonight. Is this for Cloe?"

The wolf bowed again. He walked over towards Nicolas who was still holding Cloe. Nicolas stiffened.

"He-he-hello, friend. Long time, huh?" Nicolas was so nervous around the wolf.

"Have you met before, Nicolas?" Emy came and patted the wolf as thanks.

"Yes. I believe so. Cloe was always speaking to it. I have seen him a few times in our wanderings here. But I am always so nervous around him," Nicolas stammered.

I giggled. I couldn't help it. The wolf started sniffing the blanket that Cloe was wrapped in and began rubbing up against it. He knew it was his human companion within. Her familiar had out lived her and he felt lost. The wolf tugged on the blanket. My heart went out to him.

"Nicolas, you best be bringing her over before he does it for you," I suggested.

So we placed Cloe into the wolf-dug grave by the old willow tree. A beautiful spot by daylight. But even more special now by the moonlight. I found some wildflowers nearby. I gave some to Emy and Nicolas. We each said our silent prayers and tossed them on her grave.

"So mote it be," we each said in turn. We remained standing there, lost in our own thoughts beside Cloe's grave until dawn. The wolf laid upon the grave, his head resting on his dirt covered paws. It was hard to tell, but it looked as though he was crying, too. The woods were silent out of respect for our loss.

When the sun rose, we went back up to the cottage to have some breakfast.

"I best be going home." Nicolas made his way back to his wagon.

"Stay for breakfast. I can talk to your family later if you would like," Emy offered.

Nicolas pondered the thought a moment. He shrugged. "Sounds fair enough." We all went into the cottage to start on breakfast. After breakfast, Nicholas bade us farewell for the day. He had to get things done around the village.

"I will call on you both tonight and check how you are faring?" Nicolas said on his way to his wagon.

"That will be most good of you, Nicolas. Thank you. You are always welcome here." Emy gave him some food wrapped up in a cheese cloth for lunch later.

He tipped his hat and clicked his horse to get going. We watched him go down the road.

"What do we do now, Emy?" I finally asked, never taking my eyes off of Nicolas' wagon. The wind blew at our disheveled hair and dresses.

"We wait," was her only response.

The winds felt as though they had shifted while we stood there. I smelt the salt air from the ocean upon the breeze and knew what she meant. Aaron's ship had come home. I smiled. His ship coming home meant everyone was home.

"Shall I bring the wagon around, sister?" I looked at her, smiling.

She looked back at me, giggling. "Why, yes, sister. I shan't want to walk all the way to the dock to greet our dear men home from sea. Besides, we need to bring all the goods home, too." She smirked.

We ran back to the cottage to tidy ourselves up and to tidy the cottage up as well. After all was in order in the cottage, we headed out to the wagon. Something did not feel right as we approached the wagon. I could not put my finger on it at first. I stopped short.

"What is wrong, love?" Emy's face went serious. She knew something was not sitting right with me when I did that.

"I do not know." I stared at the wagon. "Something is not right here." I scanned the area. *'What is it? Where is it? Show yourself to me,'* I said in my head. I approached the wagon bed slowly. There it was. Someone had left us a "present" in the bed of the wagon. I gasped in horror, turned away, and covered my face.

"What is wrong? What is—" Emy started. She stopped dead in her tracks. She had reached the wagon bed and saw what lay before us.

It was our lone wolf friend from the night before. There was no mistaking it. The dirt was still covering his paws. Someone had killed him and left him in the bed of our wagon during the morning while we were having breakfast or cleaning up the cottage. They had left a clean slice along his throat, from ear to ear. They had left him to bleed out. Emy held my shoulders as I quaked.

"We need to move him," she instructed, holding back tears. She wanted to sob but right now was not the time to be doing so. We had to act now and fast. We got a cloth from the cottage and rolled him onto it. Then we each took an end and carried him to the back of the cottage. We wrapped him up as best we could for now.

"His tail is missing," I noticed, and pointed it out to Emy.

"Hmmm, so it appears it is. When we see someone carrying it around, then we shall know who did this ghastly deed."

We quickly tried to clean up what blood remained in the wagon bed.

"Shall we try this again?" Emy said, trying to make light of the situation.

"Yes, let us try this again." So we got on the wagon and proceeded into the village docks to see if Aaron's ship had in fact arrived.

The ride into the village was quiet. I think we were both lost in our own thoughts. I know I was still replaying the last twenty-four hours over again in my head. I wondered if Emy was doing the same. When we reached the village, there seemed to be a commotion going on. We just tried to pretend we didn't see it. We really just wanted in and out of the village today after yesterday's chain of events.

"The witch's body is gone from the logs! You did this! You made her body disappear!" We heard shouting going on as we approached closer to the site. Emy and I looked at each other.

'What has gotten into this place?' I thought to her. *'Do they not think that we may have collected her body ourselves?'*

"You are a witch just like her! You took her so you could get any energy or power that remained in her for yourself!" another person yelled.

It was the poor girl who lived on the outskirts of the village. Her family had just moved to these parts not that long ago. They came off of Aaron's ship the last time he had come home. I looked at the crowd. *'We have to do something! She never touched Cloe's body! We did!'*

Emy stopped the wagon. She stood up in the seat. She inhaled deeply before she said anything. She scanned the villagers.

"Did it ever occur to anyone that I may have taken my sisters body for burial myself?" she yelled over the crowd.

It took a moment for the villagers to realize that someone outside of their squabble had spoken to them. They looked over at our wagon, dumbfounded.

Did they even hear her? I wondered. I saw Nicolas in the shadows. This was our chance to help her. *'Quick, Nicolas! Take the girl to safety, anywhere but here with this crowd*!' I thought to him.

He looked up at me and nodded. He ran to the girl and motioned for her to follow him.

"Let me repeat myself. Did it ever occur to anyone that I may have come after the fire had died down and removed Cloe, my sister? Physically removed her from the fire area and brought her to our home for a private burial?" Emy continued to address the crowd as Nicolas helped get the newest victim away before they tried her then and there for something we did.

Orthus walked out of the shadows. He had a menacing look upon his face. Some of the villagers had started to walk away. They knew they were wrong about what they were trying to do right then. Why had they not thought first? Of course, we would have taken our family member home for burial. Orthus stared at Emy. She glared back at him. Just before either one of them could say anything, someone else pointed to the docks.

"Look, Emy! Is that Aaron's ship docking in port?" Tabitha called out. She knew she needed to get the tension gone and fast. Everyone stopped to look. It sure was Aaron's ship. Maybe things would take a turn for the better now that the ship was back. Maybe we could put the events of the last few days –and months– behind us.

We continued to the docks. Some of the villagers came to the docks as well to greet the ship. As we stood there waiting, there was a light breeze coming in from the sea. The gulls fought over scraps a little further down as usual.

Maybe things will return to normal sooner than we thought.

Daren was standing closest to the dock, awaiting his cue. Aaron came into view. The rest of his crew stood on the sides with the rope ready in hand to toss down to tie the ship in place.

"Permission to land!" Aaron yelled from the deck.

"Permission granted! Get down here you old fool!" Daren chuckled heartily. They were close friends.

The men tossed the ropes down to the others waiting around the dock to catch them. They tied up the ship as Aaron came to shore. Emy was bursting at the seams.

"Why are you still standing here?" I nudged her to get going. Aaron shook Daren's hands and hugged him in greeting. They exchanged a few words. Then Aaron scanned the group looking for Emy. I knew when their eyes met. I felt her heart leap for joy. She felt the same as I did, that maybe things would be all better now that Aaron was home. That maybe this witch trial and burning madness would be all over now.

They ran to each other arms wide open reaching out to each other. He whirled Emy in a big sweeping circle and kissed her deeply. The rest of the villagers cheered as though this gesture finalized the end of the voyage. I smiled for them. Tears welled up in my eyes. I was glad to have something to be happy about finally. It was a shame that Cloe could not have been here still to have seen this.

"Are those tears for me, my Lady?" someone said, waking me from my thoughts. I jerked my head towards the voice.

"James!" I screeched. I threw my arms around his neck. The tears flowed even more.

"Well, now. Maybe I should be gone this long all the time," he said as he chuckled.

I sobbed even harder. I did not think that I had any more tears inside me after Cloe. But I realized they were still for Cloe.

"No, no you must not," I sobbed into his shoulder. "Cloe's dead," I blurted out. There was no better time to say it. I could not wait until we returned to the homestead to say it. The tears were not just because they were back home. They were still very much for Cloe as well.

James held me tighter. "What happened while we were gone?" he whispered in my ear. He was shocked.

'*Trial for witchcraft,*' I thought to him.

'*When did they burn her?*' he thought back to me.

"Yesterday," I spoke. I took a step back from his embrace. I looked at James. The tears were in his eyes now, too. I looked back to where Emy was with Aaron. I caught her eyes and she nodded. She had already told Aaron. James and I walked over to where they stood.

"Hey, squirt." Aaron nudged me as he always did. I managed a smile. It was good to have them home again. I just wished we had better news than this to tell on their return.

"Welcome back, brother," I nudged him back.

There was a short silence between the four of us. Seemed like time stood still for just us while everyone else around us scrambled to unload the ship. No one bothered us.

Aaron broke the silence. "We will load the wagon for you and James to bring home. We will get another wagon for the rest of what is to go home. Everything else is for market."

"Sounds like a plan, 'boss'," James smirked at Aaron.

'Keep your eyes open for anything odd like this morning,' I heard Emy think to me.

I nodded to her. *'You don't have to tell me twice,'* I thought back to her. I was uneasy about what we saw in the wagon bed earlier that day. Standing here with everyone again, it felt like it was all years behind us already. I started to feel a little light-headed suddenly. It felt almost as though someone was trying to get into my thoughts. I fought it back, hard. Maybe a little too hard.

"Why hello there, cousin!" Tabitha waltzed into the group.

BAM! It felt like I got bashed upside the head with a sack full of grain. I lost control of my balance and I fell over. I could not tell exactly what happened in those moments because it all went black. When I came to, I was lying with my head in James' lap and Emy was waving a small vial of her smelling salts under my nose.

"What happened? Are you alright?" Emy whispered to me as I came to. "Do not get up right away. Take a deep breath first."

I did as she instructed and after a few moments I was back on my feet. I noticed Tabitha standing behind everyone else with a grin across her face.

'Thank you so much, cousin. That was all the information that I needed,' Tabitha said, entering my thoughts.

I glared at her. There was a small crowd to make sure I was alright, but they seemed to be dispersing now.

'What do you mean by that, Tabitha?' I shot back at her.

"Oh nothing," she said aloud.

Emy turned on her heel, "What did you do to her, Tabitha? And don't you be playing all shy and innocent like about it, neither. I know damn well that smirk of yours means no good! Cough it up, lady!" She glared at Tabitha with those words.

Tabitha looked coyly shocked. She gasped. Her hand went up to her chest. "Why cousin, whatever could you be implying?" She tilted her head slightly and looked at Emy. She was far braver with witnesses around. She knew Emy would never lay a hand on her in any form if others were around.

Emy walked slowly and collectedly towards Tabitha. She stopped when she was nose to nose with her. She leaned over to her ear.

"I know damn well what you are up to. You may have gotten rid of Cloe that way. But rest assured, that by the Gods, I will end it here. Just remember, you are a witch just like Cloe was.

You have crossed the line, Tabitha. And for that, you will pay dearly. I don't know how yet. But that outcome lies with the fates, not with me. I will bow down and clean up the mess you have made for this family. Just like I always have in the past. But, just remember, this will be the last time I will do this for you. Next time, you will be on your own." She kissed her cheek and stepped back. All of the color had drained from Tabitha. She looked at Emy in disbelief. Only those of us closest could hear what was said between the two. The others were too far away, thankfully.

Tabitha jerked herself back to reality. She looked at me still trying to get myself together and leaning on James. There were tears in her eyes. *'I am so sorry. But I had to do it to you. You were the easiest,'* she thought to me.

'Do what? Punch me upside the head?' I snapped back at her mentally.

She looked like a hurt child being scolded for something wrong. She knew she did wrong. But *why* was the probing question at hand.

'I was told to do it.'

'By whom? Who made you do this, whatever it was?' I pushed.

She glanced towards the crowd. I dared to look in the same direction. Sure enough, hiding in the shadows, was Orthus. Hiding was not the right word. Lurking. Yes, that son of a bitch who dared call himself a servant of God was lurking in the shadows far away from the crowd, watching us. He seemed to be enjoying the scene playing out in front of him that he himself had set into motion from the very moment he first set foot into this quiet village. He was no servant of the same God as us. No. Not by far. From that point I realized he was the one who must be behind all of this. Emy was right, he must be stopped.

I looked back over at Tabitha. *'Stay away from him, Tabitha. He will get you killed as well. None of us are safe from the likes of him. None of us.'*

"I am so sorry," she said aloud and nodded to me. "And I am sorry about Cloe's familiar, too." She glanced at her toes. She took off into the crowd

"Take me home, James? I think I need to sit a little bit away from all of these eyes." I tugged his arm gently and smiled.

"Very good. We shall go as quickly as possible," James agreed.

He helped me into the wagon since I was still a little weak in the legs from all that had just occurred. My head was reeling with all that Tabitha had done and said to me. As I sat up in the wagon, I caught Emy's eyes. I nodded to her.

'He told her to do it. He has got his grip on her somehow and she cannot back out. She has made a deal with the devil, Em. It is not completely her fault. She has become his instrument to further his agenda.' I glanced over to where I had seen him last. He was still lurking there in the shadows. Was he waiting for one of us to do something? Did he really hope we were that naïve to do something here with everyone watching?

Emy nodded. "He must be stopped or it will never end."

After the wagon was loaded, James climbed aboard. He clicked the horse to get moving. We sat in silence for the ride. Did Tabitha have something to do with our finding the wolf this morning? Did she actually do that deed? Or does she just know about it?

"Are you feeling any better?" James started. I think he was tired of the silence, and a little worried considering what happened.

"A little, yes. Thank you. I am just trying to piece together what happened the last few days and what Tabitha just said to me earlier. I fear Emy may be right, and we have a much larger problem on our hands than we first thought."

"I can only imagine. Especially if Tabitha is involved in any manner. How so?" he inquired. He tilted his head with a puzzled look on his face.

"Well, for starters, I shall be needing your help when we get home. Do you remember Cloe's familiar?" With no one else around, it was a lot easier to be open about everything. It was good to have him back. I could bounce my thoughts off him. He always seemed to know what I needed.

"The wolf, right?" He thought hard. "Yes, I remember. I recall that I may have tried to shoot it one year and she practically broke my shot gun on me for doing so. After that I never went after any wolf simply because I didn't want her to go after my shot gun again. She was very mad over it."

"Yes, the wolf. And I remember that, too. She was so mad at you! I think she turned quite red in the face, too! I have never seen her madder than that day." I could not help but laugh over that thought. Tears came down my cheeks. I would never see her get mad like that again.

James stopped the wagon. He turned to me and held my hands. "What happened to Cloe's familiar?"

"We found him this morning in the bed of the wagon. He was dead." I looked into his eyes. "He was murdered. If that's the right word to use for a wolf. The throat had been slashed."

James took a deep breath. He just sat there silently. What was he thinking in there? Did he know something he was not telling me? I searched his face for any answers. I was getting desperate for normalcy again.

"There is something else. I noticed that his tail had been—" I started.

"Cut off, too?" James finished for me.

I stared at him in disbelief. How did he know? It felt like the world was pressing in on me. I needed to get out of here. '*Was she in on this, too?*' James gripped my hands a little tighter.

"I thought it was just a nightmare that I was seeing," he whispered. He wasn't really looking at me anymore. He was looking though me. Almost as though he was reliving his dream once again.

"What do you mean, James?" I ventured.

"I saw Cloe's familiar. I was there. But I was still clearly on the ship. He was lying on a pile of freshly dug dirt. There were some flowers on the ground by that old willow we all liked to go to from time to time."

"Yes, that is where we laid Cloe to rest last night. We got to the old willow and he was already there, waiting for us to arrive. He had the grave all ready for Cloe's body to be put to rest inside."

James looked a little puzzled. He knew that I could see things like this from time to time. But he had never experienced anything of the sort himself firsthand. Until now, that is. Could he be a late bloomer in the power like this? Or could someone else have planted this vision into his head? Either possibility could be very likely.

James shook his head and then continued. "He was lying upon her grave. Suddenly, he had jumped up to a standing position. He was growling deep in his throat and flashing his teeth. There seemed to be a bit of a fight or a struggle of some sort. The next thing I saw was the wolf lying upon the ground with his throat slashed open. The person was standing there with a knife in one hand, and his tail in the other. They carried him from the grave area all the way back to the cottage, then-,"

Now it was my turn to shake my head.

"Whoever has his tail is the culprit of this crime. If it can even be called that at this point. Tabitha knows something. She pretty much came out and said so today," I told him.

"Most likely so," James agreed. "Let us go back to the cottage and figure all of this out." He spurred the horse into movement again. We sat in silence for the rest of the ride, lost in our thoughts over the new information we had swapped. Once back at the cottage, we started to unload the wagon.

"You said the wolf was found this morning?" James stopped for a moment. He was trying to reevaluate the chain of events. I nodded to him. "What did you do with him?"

"This way." I led him to the backside of the cottage where we had left him covered up with some cloth. We were thinking to lay the wolf to rest next to Cloe since it was her familiar. When we got to the spot, he was not there. "What the —?" I stopped dead in my tracks. I turned towards James. "He was right here! This is where we placed him!" I cried out. "Where did he go? He was clearly dead. There is no way he could have gotten up on his own." I pointed to the spot Emy and I had left the wolf this morning before going into the village to meet up with the incoming ship. I sunk to the ground in desperate confusion. My skirt flopped everywhere. I stared at the spot the wolf had been left at.

"Where did you go, my friend?" I whispered to the wind.

James sat down next to me. I shook my head in disbelief.

"I don't understand this. Dead things do not just get up and go. Where did he go?" I whispered to the wind again. I closed my eyes and listened. I listened to the wind for any answers that it might have for me. *'Give me something to work with, I beg of thee.'*

I don't know how long we sat there for, just waiting for any answers to show themselves. I listened to the wind in the trees. I listened to the birds as they chirped and the bugs that buzzed around the gardens. The horse neighed around the front of the cottage.

Then, I saw it. Tabitha had come up to the cottage. She saw the wagon was gone. She walked to the back of the cottage. She discovered the cloth with the wolf wrapped up in it. She knelt down next to him. She uncovered and looked upon him.

"I am so sorry you had to die because of all of this," she whispered. She patted his head and wrapped him back up. She lifted the wolf up in her arms and walked away with him. I followed her in my vision. I was getting the answers I was hoping for and more. Tabitha carried the wolf down to the old willow.

"I am truly sorry you had to die. This was her favorite spot. I will place you here." She walked closer to the tree itself. She paused for a moment. Tabitha tilted her head to the left slightly. She noticed the recently dug spot where Cloe rested. But that was not why her head was tilted. She figured that we just might do that for Cloe. What had confused her was the other scene that had taken place earlier that day. The scene that led to right then.

There was blood pooled not far from the grave site. Something wicked occurred here as well. She sunk to the ground.

"Oh no," Tabitha whispered. "It was here where you died, old friend. You were watching over your familiar's grave, were you not?" Tabitha's head sunk into her hands. Her heart sobbed for such a cruelty to have taken place.

"Why so sad? You must have known this is what was going to happen. Surely, you knew that much," a masculine voice said behind her.

Tabitha lifted her head and turned towards the voice. She had anger on her face and she was ready to strike.

"This is not what was to happen! Why did you kill the wolf? He's our familiar. A friend. A protector," she said through clenched teeth.

He laughed heartily. It echoed in the forest. The animals all went silent. He seemed to be transforming in front of her. In front of me, too, though he did not know it, for now. He stood a little taller. Then, bat-like wings flapped and stretched a little behind him. What kind of creature was this? What did he have to do with Tabitha?

I breathed slowly so that I did not lose this vision. I was getting to the heart of the situation. I could not lose my focus yet.

"Tabitha, you are mine now. I told you there was no turning back once I started. You said whatever it took. This is what it takes." The creature pointed to Cloe and the wolf.

Tabitha's fists clenched tightly. So tight that her knuckles went white. She stood up slowly. "This is not whatever it takes! This is my family!" She turned around. She wanted to go after this creature. "This has gone too far! I want out!"

The creature flew to Tabitha and held her. It was so swift it took a moment to register that it had in fact moved.

"We made a deal, Tabitha. Did you forget the pact? I have come to claim my payment. Remember? Back there on that day with your sister kinfolk? They must all pay me back for that day that *you* summoned me. Especially Emy. She stopped me from fully being that day. We were so close. So close. You owe me, witch!"

The creature whispered into her ear. She stood paralyzed. The creature let her go. She dropped to the ground with a thud. Tabitha lay there slumped over the ground for a moment. While she lay there, the creature changed shape. He took on a human form again. I looked upon the eyes of Orthus, the new church worker who set up Cloe's trial, who lurked in the shadows down near the dock that day.

I gasped. My eyes flew open. I was horror stricken with my discovery. What were we going to do? Emy managed to keep this, this thing at bay once. But it had taken all of our collective powers to do so. We were one less sister now. Tabitha seemed to be stricken powerless around him herself. That may have something to do with her pact she made years ago.

"Are you alright?" James piped in through my thoughts. I jumped. I forgot he was sitting here with me still. Had he stayed right beside me this whole time? He must think I was crazy sitting here like that for so long.

I looked at James. There was only concern in his face. "What did you see?" he asked me.

"What makes you think I saw something?" I replied coyly, snapping back to reality.

"Because you always have that look on your face when something pops into your head. I think I know you long enough to know when you have seen something important and or unexpected. You had a vision."

"Oh, is that so? You know me well enough, huh?"

"Yes, yes I do, Sarah. Maybe better than you know yourself sometimes."

"Really?" I wrinkled my nose. "Then did you know I was going to do this next?" I pushed him back, got up from the ground, hitched up my skirt, and dashed across the gardens, giggling.

"What the —" James was caught off guard with that move. He realized that I had started running and he got up to follow suit. "What was that for?" he asked, running after me along the paths of the garden.

"Well, you said you knew me better than myself." I kept running around the paths, turning here, twisting there.

"That was not fair! I was only joshing with you," James said, out of breath. He finally caught up to me and grabbed my hand to stop me from running further.

"What's the matter, sea boy, can't keep up with us land folk?" I smirked and raised my eyebrows slightly.

James didn't say anything. He just held my hand slightly tighter and pulled me closer to him. His other hand wrapped around my waist, keeping me even closer. Our lips met for what seemed like forever. For a moment, I forgot about the world around us. I forgot about the trials, the burning, the vision. It was James and me. Nothing else mattered. We just stood there with our noses touching and smiling for a spell after. Just enjoying each other's company. It was nice to have him back home again.

The next thing we knew, we heard a wagon approach on the front side of the cottage. We went around to the front to see who it was. Emy and Aaron had arrived with the rest of the cargo from the ship. We helped unload both wagons since we had been distracted from doing so when we had gotten home earlier.

Emy and I started on dinner while the men finished the larger items.

"So, what did you see?" Emy asked as though I had already told her that I had had a vision quest.

"What makes you think that I saw something?" I asked her. *Does* everyone *know when I see something? Sheesh!* I thought silently.

"You just have this energy around you when you have had one, which is how I can tell."

I stood there for a moment and thought about it. "Oh, I guess I can see that happening," I replied. "The wolf was gone when we got here."

Emy stopped in her tracks. She looked at me questioningly. I held my hand up in response.

"I sat and listened. I saw that Tabitha had come and she carried him to the tree where Cloe lays now. She was going to bury him there. She had company when she got there though."

Emy stood there with that intense, motherly look on her face. "Go on," she said.

I took a deep breath. I knew she was not going to like what I was going to say next. "Remember that day by the tree with Tabitha?" I looked at Emy carefully. She nodded. "She made a pact with him, Emy. He has come for his payment for the deal she had made with him. This must have happened before we got there to stop her. That's why Cloe and the wolf are dead now. She is trying to buy her life with all of ours. Also, because we know who he really is."

"Ah, shit," was all Emy could say.

"He transformed before my eyes. You will never guess who he changed into." I pressed on.

She looked at me more intently. *'Don't say it!'* she thought. She shook her head because she was right about how evil he really was. We had to stop him and fast.

"Yes, that is exactly who it was," I spoke the words aloud.

Emy sunk in the chair closest to her. She let her head sink onto the table. "Why? Why did you have to do this, Tabitha? Even years later, I have to clean up your mess." She shook her head in her arms on the table.

I didn't know what to say or do. I just stood there for the time being watching in silence as she questioned Tabitha on the air over and over again. We couldn't just leave Tabitha here to face this mess on her own. This was not a small issue anymore. This one had turned into full evil and death. It has already taken one human life and one beloved familiar. This one was not going to be going down quietly, or easily at all. We were going to need all the help we could get.

Emy came back from her thoughts. "Tell the men dinner is ready. We will discuss this later."

"But —" I started, confused.

"We will discuss this later," she reiterated.

I knew that tone all too well. Her mind was made up. Discussion would be continued later on. Off I went to get the men.

There was not much talk at dinner time. I did notice, however, that Emy had been busy doing other things. After dinner was done, Emy and Aaron spoke in another room. So James and I went about the evening chores.

"What do you suppose they are talking about in there?" James pondered.

"You should know full well it's about the events that have just occurred within the last two days. Maybe Aaron has more information for her," I replied. '*I know* my *mind is still going over all of that right now,*' I added in my head.

James smirked. He came over towards me and wrapped his arms around me.

"Are you sure it could not be possibly anything else? They *are* married, after all." He smirked more. "I mean, we have been at sea for quite a bit of a trip this time."

I laughed, shook my head and playfully pushed him. "Oh you!"

He grabbed my hand. "Come. Let us go for a walk." He smiled and his eyes glimmered.

What is he up to now? I thought. But, I followed him anyways. I had never had anything bad happen while in the company of James.

We walked around the gardens. It was a quiet night considering the events of the day. Almost as though nothing ever happened.

"Considering all that has happened, it is a pretty good night thus far. Do you think?" James started.

"Yes, it seems pretty good, so far," I agreed. *What are you getting at James? Stop beating around the bush,* I thought.

He stopped by the bench we had under the maple tree in the yard.

"A seat, my Lady?" James gestured to the bench and bowed to me.

I raised my eyebrow. I sat down. Now I was more curious as to what he was up to. He seemed very nervous suddenly. He sat next to me on the bench.

"I have been thinking lately, especially while I was on the ship for so long, about home," he started.

Okay, I thought. *He is beating around the bush. I will give him a few moments and see if I need to jump in and save him from himself.*

"I thought about you on that ship while you were away, too," I added.

He seemed to relax slightly. He cleared his throat before continuing. "I was so glad to be home and when I saw you, I felt home."

"Aww, James. That is so sweet," I started to say.

"Hold that thought. I am not finished yet," he interrupted.

I looked at him with squinted eyes. My eyebrow rose slightly and my lips pursed. "Okay," I said, curious now.

"I felt home, because you are here. And I hope that anywhere I go that you are, that it shall always be home for me."

"What are you getting at, James?" I poked at him.

He slid off of the bench to one knee. He had a ring that he somehow pulled out without me seeing. He held it up towards me in offering. "Will you marry me?" he whispered.

It was his turn to catch me off guard. I wrapped my arms around his neck. "Yes!" I whispered back to him. He slid the ring onto my finger and twirled me around in continuous circles. We were laughing happily. After a time, we sat back on the bench.

"Is this why they snuck off to the other room?"

"Ummm… Partly," he admitted.

I nudged him. *So they knew before I knew? Those brats. Such is life.'* This was a good surprise. Some good within the bad of the last few days.

I heard a noise from the tree line. I looked at James. We sat at the ready. What came stepping through the trees was a caravan. There were wagons, horses, and people on foot. I would have recognized that wagon banner anywhere! Our gypsy family had come home to visit.

"Go get Emy and Aaron," I said, beaming ear to ear.

"Is that who I think it is?" James started.

I cut him off, pushing him towards the cottage. "Go get them, I said! Hurry up!" I chuckled and shook my head at him. James ran off to the cottage to get the others. I took my cap off and let my hair fall out of the tight bun I had it in all day. My hair flowed in the slight breeze. I waved at the caravan.

As the caravan came closer, I saw some of my kinfolk. I picked up my skirts and ran to greet them.

"Hello!" I called, waving a hand in greeting. The brunette looked at me, her long hair flowing as she walked alongside the wagon. Her face beamed as she saw that it was me. She ran towards me.

"Sarah! How glad I am to finally see a familiar face!"

We met in the middle, grab each other's hands, and twirled in our excitement.

"You couldn't have come at a better time, love," I whispered in her ear as we embraced.

She took a step back. *'He has managed to get though hasn't he?'* she thought to me. I nodded yes. *'Shit. I was afraid of this. Where are Emy and Cloe?'* she asked.

I looked deep in her brown eyes. How I had missed those deep brown eyes. Always knowing what was next.

"Emy is inside. I sent James in to get her." I took a deep breath, "Cloe, however...she's down by the old willow." I moved my eyes away.

"He has already started his work here, huh? Damn it! Too late again!" She stomped the ground. The jewels and chains of her skirt jingling about her as she did so. I grabbed her arm.

"It is not your fault, Lor. We cannot fly around to be able to stop things in time. I just realized who it was doing this a few hours ago. We've been going on for months. It took him killing Cloe's familiar for me to see who it was."

It was her turn to look deep at me. She nodded.

"You are right, my young Sarah. You always seem to know the right thing to say. We cannot fly in a blink of an eye. That I know for sure. Although it would be very handy in saving lives beforehand if we could, no?" She winked at me and smiled big.

"We'll be here for a few days at least. Make home!" Lor called out to the rest of the caravan.

We walked arm in arm up to the cottage. She felt my hand. "What is this?" She smiled at me. "How off was I on this one?" she asked about the ring.

"Tonight," I smirked. "Not too off. But you can never gauge on the time at sea." I winked and giggled.

We walked into the cottage.

"Emy! Look what the cat dragged in!" I giggled as we walked in. Emy had the water going over the fire and some food along the table.

"Cousin! It is wonderful as always to see you." Emy hugged Lor and they kissed each other on the cheek. "You have been missed terribly, my friend," she said as they stepped back from each other.

"It is good to be around familiar faces. Well, minus two, I am told?"

Emy nodded. "Just yesterday for Cloe. But, her wolf was murdered this morning sometime."

"Is it what I feared it would be? How he made his way here? Who is his main victim who gets to point the fingers?" Lor pressed on.

"Tabitha is the finger. But, it seems to be tied to who Tabitha tried to conjure up before we stopped her that day by the water. Tabitha means well deep down. But, she also wants the power to control things that she cannot be in control of. He is stronger than we originally may have thought." Emy offered up.

"I see," Lor said. She turned to me. "And you saw that in a vision today, correct?" I nodded.

"Has anyone been able to banish him from anywhere before everyone is killed?" Emy pressed.

"Not that I am aware of. We have been on his trail since we got wind of him in the area," Lor said sitting at the table. She grabbed some bread and started spreading jam on it.

"We need to figure something out soon. He has just started and Tabitha is pointing the fingers. But if things go wrong we will need to be sure to get away to safety or all will have been for nothing."

"It's been a long day, and I'm sure you are all tired from your travels. You are welcome here, as always. We shall resume this tomorrow," Emy suggested.

There was no sleep for me. My mind kept running everything around in my head. I kept playing the vision over and over again in my dreams. *'Did I miss something? There has to be something else that I am not seeing.'* I kept thinking through the night. It seemed to need some sort of energy off of us. Like it fed off of us somehow. But, he could not grab it from us as long as we were in our physical form. He could not "touch us" per se. But, once the fire touches us, we escape that physical form.

I sat up from my sleep. It seemed to click. "Vampire," I said into the dark.

Lor rolled over. "Are you alright, little Sarah?" she asked, groggily.

I jumped a little. I had forgotten she decided to stay inside with us tonight. I nudged her to wake a little better than she was. "Vampire," I told her.

"Where?" She jumped up, practically knocking me out of the bed. She was ready to defend real fast.

"No, no! I am so sorry, Lor!" I grimaced. *Whoops.* "I meant that is what we are dealing with. This thing is a type of vampire. But, he cannot touch us as long as we remain in our physical forms. He is a shape shifter. I know his human form. Tabitha does, too. He is forcing her to help him. If she does not, she dies. This is who she conjured back by the water years ago, yes. He has grown stronger since that day and is planning his revenge on all of us who stopped him from fully forming that

~ 48 ~

day. But, I am not sure. I think we need to be looking in the way of vampire to be rid of him for good. I fear we may never be rid of him unless we do."

"So you can identify him? And he walks among us?" Lor sat up straighter.

"Yes. He is in the form of the new church 'brother to be'. I think because of the things he has been doing, he can never fully obtain brotherhood status. He is doing these acts in the name of God that he would really be worshipping except for himself as I can see it thus far. I saw him lurking in the shadows today down by the port when we went to get Aaron and James. There was a squabble concerning a young girl new to town. They were trying to call her a witch. Emy distracted them as Nicolas got her away from the crowd before we had another burning on our hands."

Lor leaned back on the headboard. "It is worse than I thought." She shook her head. Her brunette hair bounced with her head as she did so. "The other towns and villages we have encountered never had much to say about what had happened there. They would just look at us and, mumble, 'The witches are gone! The women are all gone!' They would run into their homes and hide from us as we passed by. You could see the graves lined up along a far hill. Many of them would be there. We could never tell if all the women were in fact gone or not. No one would come out to talk with us."

"We must stop him before it happens here then," I whispered.

"In one village we passed through, there was a small family who lived on the outskirts. They were so far out that I almost think they were forgotten about out there. Which was probably a good thing considering the circumstances." I nodded. "They spoke a little about it. But, in hushed tones, to make sure no one else heard them just in case they started up the burnings again. She spoke of a young lad connected with the church who had come some months back. He was not quite at the brotherhood level yet. She recalled that she did not feel that with his 'position' he would ever be granted into the brotherhood with the church. He would only have the recognition of being in connection with them.

"The husband would scoff about the man, 'I never liked him. I always knew there was something strange about the lad.' He would snicker from his seat by the fire.

"One day, they heard tell that someone had accused the young lass of witchcraft. They held a trial. The new lad from the church ran the whole show. He even conducted the burning when it got to that point. He seemed to almost enjoy the poor girl screaming in pain when the fire engulfed her. 'A wicked soul is inside that lad. He is dark. You stay away from him, Jeannie, you hear?' she would tell her daughter. They hid their daughter at home. They were afraid of what might happen if he saw her. She was their only child.

"After what seemed like ages, the accusations, trials, and burnings stopped. The lad seemed to suddenly be 'relocated elsewhere'. By that time, about twenty of the women-folk in the village were burned at the stake. They even tried some of the children."

Lor rested her eyes and sat still for a moment. The whole house was hushed. Almost as though it knew she was contemplating more of her story. I broke the silence. "This type seems to be conjured or summoned forth. He cannot just come to become. I remember Tabitha was able to summon up to a point. We did manage to stop her from finishing, however. But, I wonder if one starts it up again elsewhere, or if another person did the same summoning spell, would it just pick up where the previous one left off? Unknown to the new summoner? So that he just builds fuel until he is strong enough to remain no matter what? And if he is in fact enjoying those he manages to convince others to try to have burned, is he feeding off of those life essences? Is that how he stays strong enough to stay here on our plane of existence?" I was rattling off questions a mile a minute.

Lor thought on these.

"All very good questions, Sarah." She contemplated some more over them. "If it is in fact a type of vampire, then we need to be looking into how to protect and then attack to vanquish."

"That does sound like a very logical way to go. But, I feel that this particular one will be anticipating just that. He already has Tabitha. For all we know, he may have made her do up a charm of some sort to keep us from protecting those in the village," I added.

"And because she is blood, it may be harder to counteract it. Especially if it is Tabitha. She tends to play around with hers in some form. There seems to always be, shall we say, levels of complexity to her stuff," Lor added.

I nodded. It seemed when Tabitha was involved, things got more difficult for us. Maybe it was a way of challenging us to think more into how we did things ourselves. Or maybe, she didn't even realize she was doing it as such. I never knew.

"We will need to share this with Emy in the morning," I said.

In the morning, Lor and I found Emy outside in the gardens. Something did not seem right. The air had changed somehow. Emy was standing very still. Almost as though she was a statue. I looked closely at her face. I waved my hand in front of her eyes.

"Emy. Earth to Emy. Are you in there? Hello?" I softly said to her. Nothing. *Hmmm. That always seemed to work before.* I looked at Lor. I shrugged my shoulders.

"That has always worked before. I wonder if she is further away than usual," I told Lor.

Lor looked around. Nothing out of the ordinary around the grounds. She stepped beside me. She took my hand and Emy's hand and motioned me to do the same. We stood there, the three of us, quietly. After a few moments, Emy opened her eyes. She started to waver. But, since we had her hands already, we caught her to keep her from falling over.

We sat her gently onto the ground. We said nothing. We gave her time to collect her bearings at being back in her body and back on the grounds at home. After a short time, Emy looked at us in recognition.

"So where did you go?" I asked finally.

Emy took a moment before answering. "I went to another village." She stared off into the distance. She was trance-like. "He had been there prior. So much sorrow. So many graves. So many, so many..." She drifted off.

Lor and I looked at each other.

"What did you do there, sweetie?" Lor whispered to her. We did not want to startle her in case she had more to share. Sometimes one forgets all of the details from a vision quest if not shared right away.

"An older woman saw me," she continued. She seemed puzzled by this. "She said to watch out for the demon that dwells in the church now. She could not help anyone by herself she told me. She said the poor girls never stood a chance against him. He would nod to another girl and his "chosen one" would accuse her of witch craft. Many different things, from killing off a crop to making someone fall in love with another."

Emy shook her head. "The woman had a spell, a potion to use to be rid of him. But, she said she was not strong enough to perform the task on her own. 'You have sisters, do you not?' the woman asked me. 'You must all work together on this. I will send you the items. You will know what to do with all of it.' The woman walked across her home smiling. 'You three will finish what I could not handle myself. You already know what to do. Yes, yes. You my child already know what needs to be done.' That was when I came back here," Emy finished.

We sat there silently for a time. We were all rolling this over in our heads.

"How does she know where to send it to?" I pondered out loud.

"If she was not scared when she saw Emy, then she is one of us. And she just knows. You know how that works, Sarah. Do you really need to ask that one?" Lor smirked and looked at me.

"Hey, it was just a thought. Sheesh, can't a girl think out loud?" I playfully shoved her.

"Either way, we need to figure out just what we need to be doing about this whole mess. I fear there will not be much time if he has already set the wheels into motion," Emy added.

We went into Lor's wagon to look into her library. There were books she acquired during her travels and some she had written over time. She had travelled far and wide, so she had all kinds of information within their bindings. It was quiet within the walls of the wagon. The plush velvet and satin pillows I sat upon made me feel safe. For a moment, I almost forgot that Cloe had died. Almost. I was half hoping she would be walking in through the door to help us read through everything. But, she never did. The nightmare was still very much real.

After a time, I closed my eyes. I could not even gauge how long we had been at all of those books. I had a tall pile beside me that I had already gone through. My eyes were tired of reading. I dozed off for a bit. It was broken with various memories over the past few days. Of Cloe burning, her silent screams still resonating within my head as though the fire was still going on. I saw Orthus, standing beside the fire against them. He seemed exhilarated by the fire and by Cloe dying.

'Why are you so happy about this?' I wondered in my dream. 'What are you feeding off of to keep you going; to keep you so strong in power?' I dared further into my dream. I needed more information on him. Cloe's screams had finally died down. I saw her soul eave her physical form. She shone bright yellow. She was heading to the next realm. But, she never made it there. I saw Orthus watching her ever so closely. As soon as she was fully separated from her body, the demon within him removed

~ 54 ~

itself from his physical form and absorbed her. She became lost within his energy. He glowed yellow from her essence. Now, she would never be waiting to welcome us on the other side. Not unless we destroy him. I wondered if all of those taken by him would be released if we vanquished him entirely.

Then I saw Tabitha by the water with the wolf carried in her arms. I could smell the death on him. It made me sick to my stomach to smell that. Orthus' eyes glowed with hunger. He needed more energy to be complete. He was not fully transformed into the physical realm. We still had time before he was complete. But exactly how much longer did we have? How many more had to die before that happened? It was apparent that he could not physically get us in this realm. We had to be separated from our physical form before he could touch us. I wondered if we did something to our essence, if we could get him that way for an attack.

Then, to the time the ship came in. How we stopped the villagers from going after Samie. I saw how he was in the shadows, feeding off of the negative energy. He seemed to have glared when I held onto James and Emy held onto Aaron. I saw him glow black around his human frame. Why was us holding the men like that making him so angry? I couldn't understand.

I tossed on the pillows. I could not get comfortable all of a sudden. Then, I saw as I knocked over a pile of books beside me, the young girl from the village. She was in the roof bedroom, crying silently. She hid under the blankets on her bed and listened closely.

"I told you! There is no girl child that lives here! Now you be gone from here!" her father bellowed from below. He was trying to force the intruder out of his home to no avail.

She dared not breathe for fear of being found. She heard whispers below. Were there more than one intruder?

"Then it must have been *you* who was seen in the village the other day! If there is no girl who lives here, then *you*, lady, must be the witch! You would have been able to transform into different shapes and sizes. How do we know that you yourself are not really that little girl everyone keeps seeing in the village?" Tabitha's voice resonated throughout their cottage.

'Oh, Tabitha! Why do you still have to be involved in this whole mess?' I thought sadly.

"We must bring her in for viewing and questioning right away. There are to be no delays this time. If you really are not a shape shifting witch, then you will be cleared. Nicolas, remove this woman from this cottage and put her to the wagon now," a man's voice rang out. I recognized the voice. It was Orthus. He wanted that little girl so badly. She must be one of us. Is this happening right now? Has it already occurred? My eyes flew open.

I jumped up from the pillows I was sleeping on. The books all fell every which way as I did.

"What the —" Emy started.

"Is everything alright, Sarah?" Lor asked.

They were both very much startled by my sudden flight off of the pillows. I stopped almost in midflight to the door. "We must leave. We must go right way! There isn't much time! They are after the girl! They have taken her mother instead. We must collect the child and bring her here for safety. We must act now!" I stammered.

They stared at me, shocked.

Emy stood up slowly. "Hold on, sweetie," she started quietly as though she was speaking to a skittish horse spooked by its own shadow. "Do you mean the new family?"

I nodded.

"Who was there?"

Tabitha, Nicolas, and..." I started.

"I was afraid of this," Lor piped in.

They looked at each other, then at me.

"To the wagon, fast." Emy pointed to the door.

We raced across the way to the wagon that was already waiting. Aaron looked up from his work of chopping the wood. He cocked his head to one side.

"Is everything alright, Love?" he asked Emy.

"I do not know as of yet, dear. I hope to the heavens so. But, you will know when we return. Just hope that there is one extra for dinner tonight."

"Have a safe travel then." He kissed her third eye for safe leave. Aaron stood and waved us off. I saw James come around from the back of the cottage with more wood for Aaron to chop.

'We will be back soon, I hope. I will explain later, promise.' I thought to James directly. I was not sure if he had heard my thought to him or not. But, that will have to wait until we return.

The horses sped down the worn path through the woods. This family lived on the out skirts of the village like us. That way they would not to be disturbed by nosy village folk with all of their gossip. The forest raced past us as we ran the horse down the road. There was no way to tell when my vision was going to take place or if it had already taken place. Finally, we saw the clearing up ahead for their homestead. As we came up the hill closer to the house, all seemed quiet.

"Maybe it has not happened yet?" I said, hopeful.

"We shall see once we get inside," Emy replied.

We pulled up to the house. All was quiet. We got off of the wagon and slowly walked up to the door. We looked at each other. Emy knocked on the door. There were whispers before someone came to the door. A man answered.

"Are you alright? Is everyone here still here?" Emy asked bluntly.

'Way to beat around the bush,' I thought to her.

Emy shot me a look.

"Are you alone?" he asked quietly through the slightly opened door.

We nodded. He opened the door more to let us in. Inside, the fire was crackling and breakfast was still on the table. It was eerily quiet inside the house. I looked at Emy, worried.

'We are too late,' I thought to her sadly.

Emy raised her hand to hush me. "May we sit?" she asked calmly. He nodded and sat at the head of the table.

"They took her yesterday." He looked at his fingers as he twirled a small trinket around them.

"We know. That is why we are here. Is your daughter still safe?" I said.

He looked up at me and tilted his head. "How do you know about this?"

"She saw it. Also, we stopped them from attacking your daughter in the village," Emy replied.

"Ah. So you are the ones who helped her escape. Thank you for that." He felt relieved. But, what was the more pressing issue was the further safety of his daughter.

"Where is she now?" Emy asked.

The girl emerged from the room she had been hiding in.

"I am here," she answered quietly.

We all turned towards her. She was not the little girl like we saw back in the village. She held her head high and held her composure, considering what had happened earlier on. She grew up a little over the last few days. I stood up and hugged her.

"Thank God you are alright," I whispered in her ear.

She stepped away from me and looked at all of us then took a seat. I sat back down at the table next to her. I was relieved we could at least save one of them.

~ 59 ~

"My mother will not be coming back, will she?" she asked calmly.

"No. More than likely she will not. However," Emy paused for a moment to look up at her father, "with everyone's permission, I feel that we need to remove you from the home for your safety."

The father nodded. He understood completely. The girl looked at Emy. I could feel the tension building up within her.

"What do you mean?" she asked, scared of what the answer would be.

"I feel that you should come with us to our home and hide there. Our gypsy family has arrived for a visit and we can have you stay with them either until this passes or we need to all leave together. But, at least we can keep you alive this way."

'A perfect plan!' I thought to Emy.

"Yes, this is an excellent plan," I said, "We can have you pretend to be one of our gypsy family members and if things continue to get worse, you can leave with them! Then, your father can meet up with you later on." I smiled to try and reassure her it was the right thing to do. Deep in my head I hoped this plan of Emy's would work. We silently waited for her response. It seemed like hours before she finally spoke.

"What about you, father? Will you be alright alone?" she asked him.

"Of course, daughter, knowing that you are safe and protected will make me feel secure with anything else that comes my way," was his answer.

She nodded at that. "Then, I will go with you."

"Perfect. Go ahead and get your things. Try to take mainly your personal things. You will not need much clothing, although, the more of your items you take with you the better your family can keep up with the 'we do not have a daughter' act. This way, if they do search the house, there will be nothing for them to find that they were lying," Emy instructed.

So we packed the girl up. When everything was loaded, we left her and her father alone to say their goodbyes. We handed her a cloak.

"Put this on, dear. Raise the hood over your face and whatever happens, never lift it off of your face until we are in safety," I instructed her.

She nodded and did as she was instructed.

"Only come to us if you absolutely must. Otherwise we may lose this fight," Emy told the father. "If we must, we can set up secret meetings for better safety. But, as you have never had a need to come to us before in the past, it will look highly suspicious if you started doing so now. Focus on your wife."

He nodded. With that, we sped off into the night back through the woods, back to the safety of the cottage.

When we got back to the cottage, Aaron, James, and Lor ran outside to greet us in anticipation. We looked around to make sure nothing was out of the ordinary. We helped the girl out of the wagon and Lor ran her inside the cottage. Aaron helped Emy, and James helped me off of the wagon.

"Did everything go alright?" Aaron asked.

"Yes, we will discuss this more inside, though. Too many ears out here," Emy replied.

"Dinner is set on the table and waiting," James said, trying to pretend to change the subject.

Emy nodded and smiled at him. "Thank you for tending to that for me."

We went inside the cottage to sit and eat dinner. I was a solemn and silent meal. No one really knew what to say. We were all lost in our thoughts. And who could blame us? After the last few days of events, my head was ready to explode with everything that I had racing around inside it.

After dinner was over, Emy asked the men to gather our guest's belongings from the wagon. I showed the girl my room since no one was ready to enter Cloe's room yet. It was still too soon to do that.

"I am sorry about Miss Cloe," the girl said, attempting to start a conversation.

"It was not your fault. You did not point the finger at her, did you?" I replied.

She shook her head no.

"What is your name? I mean, since you will be staying with us for some time, we should know each other's names," I continued with a smile.

She nodded and returned the smile." My name is Samantha. My mother calls me Samie." She drifted off to her own thoughts with this. She had such sadness in her eyes. I could feel the pain she felt within. Who could blame her? Her mother was taken for a witch trial and we removed her from the only other family to protect her. We just lost our own sister. We understood this pain. But we also knew that you need to just press on when things get like this.

I finished filling one of the dressers with her clothes. "Well, I believe that will do it." I turned and looked at Samie. "Shall we proceed back to the others and see what is next on the agenda?" I winked at her.

She smiled. "Yes. I think that I shall like to do that."

So we went down to the kitchen area to see what the others were doing. Emy and Aaron were sitting at the table. They stopped talking when Samie and I entered the room. They must have been discussing Samie's stay here and how we were going to be protecting her.

"Did you get settled in alright?" Emy asked.

"Yes. Everything went smoothly. Her name is Samie," I answered.

"Very good. Welcome to our home, Samie. Because of the circumstances, this is to be your home now, too. So feel free to roam anywhere on the grounds. You are not a prisoner here by any means. But I do ask that you try to stay as close to the cottage as possible unless you are with one of us. Otherwise our effort in keeping you safe will have been in vain," Emy instructed.

"Yes ma'am," Samie answered. She had questions in her eyes.

"Sit, child." Emy motioned at a chair near her. I took the other seat. "As it is evening, there will be nothing we can do for your mother tonight. In the morning, you will stay here and help Sarah with any work around the cottage. My husband, Aaron, and I will go into the village on business and see what we can find out. I hope that we still have an ally on the inside. We will see what they have done to your mother thus far and try to see if we can do anything yet about it."

Samie and I nodded. So we get stuck at home.

"Maybe I can show you around the gardens tomorrow?" I suggested cheerily.

"That would be lovely, Sarah. Thank you. I have heard so much from the villagers about your gardens. I have always hoped to see them first hand." Samie smiled sweetly.

'Maybe we can make it a little happier about having to come here with us,' I thought to Emy.

'Just keep an eye on her. See what powers she might be holding within her. They wanted her, not her mother. They think she has some form of powers or they would not have been looking for her. It will not take long for them to realize they took the wrong one. Unless her mother has powers, too,' she thought back to me.

I nodded and smiled. A bigger job than I thought. I can handle this. We said our good-nights and went off to our beds. It was such a long day with all the new information. My head was beginning to swim from it all.

Tomorrow is another day, I thought to myself. *We will continue the search for answers then.*

"Very well then, I am pretty tired myself. Where shall we be looking for answers when we do go looking?" Samie asked.

I turned towards her, shocked. *How could she have known what I was just thinking?* I just stared at her, suddenly nervous. *Could this have been a trick of Tabitha's? Has Orthus sent a younger one into his plans to get at us more easily?*

Samie waved her hands up in the air. "Uncle," she said jokingly. "I have the gift, like you. It is true. My mother is not as strong in the gift as I am. I can read thoughts, most of the time." She trailed off into her thoughts.

I sat on the edge of the bed and looked at Samie. "Why did you not tell us about it as soon as you got here?" I asked.

Samie sat next to me. She sighed heavily. "I was not sure if you had the gift, too. I also wanted to make sure you really were on my side. That you wanted to keep me...safe." She paused at the end. She looked at me like a scared mouse in front of a cat licking its lips for the meal fresh in front of him. I hugged her.

"Baby, we are on your side, most definitely! Our own sister was just murdered. Our cousin however is not on our side. We must tread lightly around Tabitha. I knew your mother was taken. That I had seen while I slept. That is why we came to collect you."

"You saw me? When?" Samie was now curious that I had a different gift other than what her and her mother had.

"I see things. Visions, actually. This particular one was about you. I saw because I was so exhausted from reading so many books in our research. I rested my eyes for a short period of time. I saw other things as well. But, when I had gotten to you, I snapped awake and knocked everything around me over. We raced to you in hope that it had not happened yet."

"I see. Can you control what you see? Or do they just come? I had to learn how to control listening to everyone's thoughts. Sometimes I could not sleep because my parents would let their thoughts run. I would stay up until I knew they were sleeping. Then, I would sleep." Samie looked sad when she spoke about her parents.

It must be hard to be away from them, I thought to myself. *I hope we can figure out this problem quickly. And I hope Samie can at least be able to be back with her father. I do not see them delaying things with her mother however.*

Samie looked up at me with sad eyes. She heard my thought. "I'm sorry, Samie. But from what we know about these people, they want to clear everyone related to this as quickly as possible."

"I understand. There is probably no hope in saving my mother. But at least I can be saved from the same fate," Samie said solemnly. The poor girl was wise beyond her years. She understood all of this very quickly. No wonder they wanted her. I wondered if she might be the key for us to be able to dispose of this demon altogether for good.

We said our good nights and went to bed. I tossed during the night. I do not remember my dreams. I woke from time to time to find Samie tossing in her sleep as well. In the morning, I nudged her.

"Hey, Samie, we may as well get up. The sun is starting to rise. I do not see either of us getting much rest at this point.

Samie opened her eyes. "I do not think I got any sleep this night. I agree with you. Let us go see what today will bring, shall we?"

So we got up from the bed and got ready for the day. We went down to the kitchen and started on the morning chores. Emy was already up and getting things ready for Aaron and her to go into the village for their snooping venture.

"Couldn't sleep either, I see?" Emy asked as we entered the room. We nodded to her. We helped Emy get things ready for the day. Emy looked at me at one point. *'Did you find out her power? Why did they want this girl so badly?'* Emy thought to me.

"Samie, here, can read thoughts. She has learnt some control over this gift but it can still be troubling at times," I spoke aloud to Emy.

Emy stared at me. I wrinkled my nose. "It is pointless for our conversations to not be out and open around her. She will hear it all regardless."

Emy put her kneading down. She wiped her hands on her apron. "I see." She walked over to Samie and placed her hand on Samie's shoulder. Samie went tense. "Come sit down, child. I will not hurt you. But there are other ways to control your gift so you do not fall prey to any unwanted trouble," she explained softly. "There are rules set in place in this family of which you will learn to abide by. We will help teach you how to control your gift so that you may be able to better follow our first rule."

Samie's eyebrow rose as though she was going to pose a question to Emy.

"Sit, child! Sit. We will get through your first lesson a whole lot more quickly if you get them there little legs of yours moving."

I chuckled and took a seat myself. I had to watch this. Emy went all school teacher on this girl as though she was one of the family. I remember those days when we were growing up.

Emy looked at me. "You can finish the bread, Sarah."

Dang. Busted, I thought.

It was Samie's turn to chuckle. Then Samie went hushed and sat up straighter. Emy had scolded her with the thought. Lessons had begun for Samie. Bread baking I went. I listened as Emy and Samie would speak occasionally as I kneaded the bread and placed each onto the side hearth to bake.

When I finished, I wiped my hands. "Are you set in here if I tend the gardens?" I asked Emy.

"Yes. Samie and I can finish in here. Can you see to eggs first?" Emy replied.

Samie seemed deep in concentration when I left the cottage. I strolled over to the chicken coop to see if there were any eggs to be had. The sun was just starting to peek over the horizon. There was a cool, crisp mist that had settled around the homestead.

I approached the chicken coop. Something did not feel right, almost as though there was something else there. The mist lifted slightly as I got closer to the entrance for the coop. My heart went to my throat. There was blood along the ground of the coop entry.

"What in the world?" I started. I stared at the blood and visually tried to follow the trail to see where it went to. The trail led straight into the entrance of the coop itself. I opened the small gate and stepped into the area. I walked slowly and quietly to the coop. There was no sound from the coop. Not a single chicken clucked. I remember that I didn't even hear the rooster crow this morning. He was usually up by now. I poked my head into the coop.

I screamed. I dropped my basket, hitched up my skirts, and ran back to the cottage. Emy and Samie came out of the cottage upon my screams. Aaron and James came trailing behind them.

"What is it, dear?" Emy stopped me.

I breathed heavily. I pointed to the coop that I had just run from.

"They're, they're...dead," I gasped in between breaths. "Every one of them are gone." I looked at Emy. She showed concern in her face. She knew that there was something more. Something I did not dare say out loud, and with our new addition, not think.

"Aaron, take James and search the coop. I will take everyone else inside for safety." Emy gave Aaron a look.

'Ask me no questions and I will tell you no lies. At least not around our friend,' I thought to Emy.

Emy shuffled Samie back inside the cottage. We started to do busy work to keep us and our thoughts otherwise occupied.

"What are you not sharing with me?" Samie finally demanded. "Why have I not heard a single thought from either of you this entire time?" She sounded desperate.

I looked at Samie, then at Emy. My eyes went to the floor. I closed them to brace for impact. I opened them backup, slowly. Staring back at me were Samie's big brown eyes. They were brimming with tears. I could not keep this from her any longer.

'I cannot do it, Emy,' I thought desperately. 'She needs to know. So she can understand the situation, completely.'

Emy walked closer.

"It was not just the chickens that were slaughtered inside the coop," I stared. "There was something else in there as well. I would not have screamed like that if it was just the chickens. We're dealing with something a lot stronger than we thought; a lot more evil than we have planned on. They know we have information on them. We also have what they want. Samie, you must stay inside for the moment. You must not show any form of acknowledgement of what I found in there. If you do, they will win," I begged her before I dared to tell her further. I searched her eyes to see if she heard anything I had just said.

"Samie, why don't you have a seat for a moment?" Emy touched her shoulders as to guide her to a chair. We had a feeling that those involved would be watching for reactions so they could pounce at finding Samie. To have stooped this low was gutsy at best. We hoped Samie would stay with us until we could really tell her in safety.

Samie's eyes were blank. She seemed to be lost in thought.

"Emy, we need to snap her back to us, and quickly. She's searching for answers with Aaron and James," I realized.

But, it was too late.

Samie sprang to life suddenly. "Father!" she yelled. She bolted for the door. We were not fast enough to stop her. She was already racing to where Aaron and James were.

They had managed to move his body to the wagon bed for a private burial later on. Samie sobbed. She looked at Emy and me as we caught up to her. Then, she turned and ran into the woods.

'No, don't separate from us! That is exactly what they want! You. Alone!' I thought desperately. I hitched up my skirts and ran after her. She ran long and hard. Finally, Samie stopped and turned towards me.

"Why? Why did they kill him? Why do they want my mother? Why do they want me? Why not let them have me? Why did you take me with you? What am I so important?" she screamed at me.

I saw the pain and the anger radiate off of her.

"Sweetie, I took you to keep you safe, to protect you. That is my job; to keep you alive and away from them. They killed your father to get to you. They took your mother because they thought she was as powerful as you are," I whispered to her. This was the only way I knew to calm her down. She was glowing red all around herself. I did not dare enter her personal bubble as of yet. That would pose a risk to everyone.

"His death will not be in vain. I promise you this." I tried to search her eyes for acknowledgement. I searched for a way to get through.

"You do not know what it is like to lose everyone!" Samie screamed. She threw her hands up into the air.

I stepped close towards her. Now I was mad. "I don't know?! I don't know? Let me ask you something, little girl. Do you know what it is like to sit there and watch your own sister burn? Do you know what it is like to feel? And I mean FEEL them like she does? To feel those flames that stole her life from her? She screamed in agony from those flames! She is still there screaming!" I felt hot all over.

Samie looked at me. The red changed to a light orange. Her arms went back down to her sides. I had gotten through the wall. She realized now just how connected we truly were. We were her family now. Whether she wanted us or not, we needed to protect her at all costs. We needed to protect her from the brutal way her father died.

Samie slowly sunk to the ground. I sat next to her. Her head rested on my lap and she cried. I stroked her hair. The energy she had built up slowly released itself from her as she let go. We just sat there like that. Emy sat on the other side of Samie and rubbed her back. When Samie's sobs quieted down enough, I spoke to her. "It is alright to be mad and to cry. Get mad all you want. But don't get mad at us. We did not want this any more than you do. We did not want Cloe or your father to die. When we saw them attacking you back in the village we knew they would not be stopping any time soon. We need to bond together or they will never be stopped. He wants you. That has been made very clear this morning with your father. He will do anything. Anything."

I stood up quickly. I felt another presence around us. We were not alone here. I slowly turned around in a circle, scanning the area around me. *'Run. Run fast and run now!'* I thought out. Samie and Emy sprang up from the ground. We grabbed hands and sprinted as quickly as we could.

I couldn't tell you from which direction he had come from. We got knocked to the ground. Samie screamed. I felt her grip loosen from my hand.

"NO YOU DON'T!" I commanded.

Emy still held Samie in her other hand. I managed to get back up on my feet. It was Orthus. He came to collect her himself. I stood with a glare of death in my eyes. I lifted my hands up to my chest in a prayer. I breathed deeply and slowly while I closed my eyes. I snapped them open and threw my arms to my sides straight out.

"YOU WILL NOT TAKE THIS ONE. SHE BELONGS TO ME!" I commanded at him.

Orthus fell to the ground and loosened his grip on Samie.

"Run!" I yelled to Emy and Samie. My eyes never left him. I wanted to keep him down.

"What about you?" Samie started.

"She can take care of herself, let us be gone from here." Emy pulled her away.

Orthus watched them run off. His eyes moved to me.

"You little witch! You will pay for that." Orthus glared at me. His eyes glowed red. I stood my ground. Again my eyes never left him.

"She belongs to me. You and your kind will not have her. You will never touch her. Go from this place. You are not welcomed on these grounds." I watched him. I focused all of my energy on keeping him down long enough for Emy to get away with Samie. We stood there, I pushed him down while he fought back to move.

"Father! Leave them alone. Have you not done enough already for one day?" Nicolas' voice pierced the silence between us like a knife cutting through butter.

His voice caught me off guard and broke my concentration. Orthus broke free. I watched in shock.

Damn it! I thought. *I am still not strong enough!*

Orthus tried to transform into his other shape. Nicolas was standing in front of him now. He reached his hand out and touched his father's shoulder. "No, Father. Not today." Nicolas looked at his father.

Orthus stared at his son. He could have killed me there on the spot. Nicolas could have helped him. But, Nicolas was not on their side on that. To this day I thank the Gods that that was the case. Nicolas seemed to have had enough power over his father to have stopped him. At least for now.

Orthus turned back towards me. "This is far from done, witch. I will have that girl. And none of you will stop me," he said. He looked back at Nicolas. "NONE of you." He changed and flew off on his bat-like wings.

~ 74 ~

Nicolas turned towards me. That drained me of all of my energy that I fell to my knees. Nicolas ran to my side.

"Are you alright?" he asked me, concerned.

I shook my head slowly. "I will be fine in a while. Will you help me back home?"

"Certainly, Sarah. I will help in any way that I can."

"May I ask you something?" I said to him.

"Sure. You can ask me anything. I have nothing to hide from you; just like I had nothing to hide from Cloe," he replied.

"Why?" was all I could think of.

"Why what, Sarah?" he asked, confused.

"Why are you helping us? Why did you stop him? Are you not one of them?"

He looked as though I had slapped him in the face with those questions. He took a moment to gather his thoughts. Then, he spoke. "I am sorry that you are confused. I do not mean for you to be so. I do not feel like my father and brother do. I am content with our own deep magic. I do not need someone else's. And I certainly do not want eternal life. They have become out of control and honestly, I am tired. I will help you in any way that I can."

I thought about what he said. We were all tired of fighting. We can only do so much.

"Fair enough of an answer," I said.

We shall see when we get home if he is telling the truth. Samie will know what lies beneath, I thought to myself. *I am still unsure if we should trust him fully as of yet.*

We finally reached the cottage. Emy had been waiting by the door, watching. She ducked inside and told something to someone. She opened the door and James came running out. When he reached us, James had a look on his face towards Nicolas.

"It is alright, James. Nicolas stopped his father from doing anything further, for now. Orthus is not very happy with either of us right now," I assured him.

He still looked at Nicolas. "Are you certain of this?" he asked me.

"Positive. After all, he was going to ask for Cloe's hand." I walked away from the two of them and into the doorway. They both stopped. Their faces said it all. They were both surprised and shocked that I had said that. I looked back at them. "You may want to close your mouths before the bugs land in them. I know, yes. That's what I do." I shrugged my shoulders and went inside. They followed suit.

Inside, we all sat around the table. No one spoke. *Are we all afraid to say what needs to be said?* I thought.

'Sorry, I am assessing Nicolas right now. When did he show up?' Samie piped into my thoughts.

I looked over at her and nodded. *'Does he seem true in being on our side?'* I thought back to her.

She wrinkled her nose and raised her eye brow. *'Seems to be, so far.'*

I breathed in deep. *'Here goes nothing,'* I thought to her.

"Nicolas stopped his father for me today. He sent him away. Nicolas has offered us his help in any way that he may." I broke the ice. I tossed out the first stone. Let's see if anyone else joins me.

"What does your family want with us?" Emy asked Nicolas finally.

Nicolas sat there a moment in thought.

'Read him, Samie. If something does not add up, call him on it,' I thought to Samie.

'On it,' she answered back with a nod.

"With you, it is your book. But he will never be able to open it without you. So he needs one of you as well. He will not tell me why he needs Samie so badly though. He cannot physically get any of you as of yet though. Even with Cloe's essence, I do not feel that that is enough to give him the power to be able to physically get anyone at all," Nicolas said. He glanced around the room.

'He seems true to his word,' Samie thought at me.

"He feeds off the essence to grow in power," Nicolas continued. "But, he cannot touch anyone to get it from them. He has to wait until they are dead and leaving their body before he can do so. The stronger they are, the more powerful he becomes."

"If he is already fairly strong, then why could you stop him earlier?" I asked him.

"You were already holding him down. I just added to your doing. Combined we were stronger. Combined, you will all be strongest." Nicolas sat back in his chair. He seemed to be a little more at ease.

"You cannot keep living like this. You have had enough." Samie looked at us. Nicolas agreed.

"The bigger concern at hand is how we can stop him. And I mean for good. We cannot afford to have him keep coming back. Nicolas you may be able to help by giving us insight on your father better than we already have. I believe Samie is our key to getting rid of him for good. I am not sure yet on how. If combined, we are strongest; then, by the Gods, we will do just that," Emy informed the rest of us.

"Let us be going, Samie. I know what that means," I said, standing up from my seat. James stood up as well.

"I will go with you, just in case you need a hand with anything," James offered.

"What does she mean?" Samie asked.

Lor stood up, too. She sighed. "It means we are hitting the books, again."

Samie raised her eye brows.

"We don't know it all. We have to go read up on stuff and see what we can find to help us." I took her hand and we left the cottage. As we left, I heard Nicolas still speaking with Emy.

"I am not sure if I may be allowed to return home after what I did here today," he confessed.

"We will cross that bridge when we come to it. Do not worry your head over that one," Emy comforted.

That was all I heard before we closed the door behind us. We climbed into Lor's wagon to resume our "research."

"Wow. This is not at all what I expected to be inside here. It is simply beautiful." Samie stared in amazement.

"Why, thank you, child," Lor said, smiling. "Not many get to see the inside of my wagon unless they are family. And for one so new to us, it means a lot."

"Thank you for allowing me to see it." Samie bowed towards Lor out of respect.

I smiled at the conversation between the two. Then, I turned to my former pile of pillows and dove on top of them. I sunk in to the plush silky pillows. The soft feathers within them pushed down as I landed on them and released the aromas that were hidden within them. I closed my eyes and imagined I was elsewhere.

"Sarah!" Lor broke into my stolen moment of solitude.

I sat upright, frowning. "What?"

"Do not be diving into my pillows," she scolded me with her hands on her hips.

"Well, how else can I get the smells out of them?" I frowned at her, my lower lip quivering.

We both burst out into laughter. Samie looked at us, confused.

"It is what we do. You will come to expect it," Lor explained, still laughing.

Samie just gave us both a look and shook her head. "I feel there is a lot more than just that which I will need to come to expect. What do we need to be looking for? And what does Orthus from church have to do with all of this?"

Lor and I looked at each other. I nodded and took a deep breath. "Orthus is part of the church, yes. But he is faking, so to speak. He and his family in fact are all vampires. He is posing as someone from the church to cover his actions. Everything he does is in the name of God. But it is not for the one God everyone else thinks it is," I said.

"I follow you so far," Samie said.

I continued, "This way, he can go around heading up all of these witch hunts whenever he chooses. He knows who he needs. He will then find someone within the village to accuse that person of witch craft and it escalates from there."

Samie nodded that she still understood.

"We had stopped him once before, years ago. Or so we thought that we did. But, I guess we really just delayed him access here until now. He has been trying to get a hold of our family book for years. We have something in there that he needs. Either we already know how to get rid of him, or it is how to make him much more powerful than he is now. He cannot take our essence unless it has left our bodies once we die; thus the burnings. He can publically be there at the death.

And no one is the wiser that he has taken the most sacred part of a human life."

"The soul," Samie whispered.

I nodded. "Correct. There in lays the rebirth and regeneration of one to another life. To also guide future loved ones to the other side as well. Cloe will not be there. Not at this time. But, maybe there is a way I can have those he has stolen expelled from him."

Lor jumped in, "Then we can give him a good punch that will send him gone for good?"

I nodded. It all became clear as to what we needed to do.

"This is where I come into play," Samie added.

We both stopped dead. We looked at her. It was our turn to be confused.

"How do you think, darling?" I asked.

She thought a moment, gathering the words for us to understand before speaking. For such a young age, she seemed to have grown over these last few days at such a fast pace.

"Well, I seem to be the strongest out of all of us as far as any of us can tell. Correct?"

"I guess so." I shrugged.

She started pacing back and forth. "So then, if this Orthus, as we call him, really does feed off of our essence when we have died, we need to attack him as he tries to get us. Do you still follow me?" She stopped a moment and looked at me to make sure I was reading her correctly.

"I think so." I narrowed my eyes at her to think clearly. "You know that we cannot possibly ever let him have you at the stake though. Are we clear on that?" I finished.

She started to rebut at me and I held up my finger. "Hear me out first. If it all goes wrong when you went to do whatever then we are all in grave danger and any glimmer of hope to get rid of him will be lost for all human kind."

"Understood. But, who then would be strong enough to do this in my place?" Samie proceeded to reevaluate the terms.

"I will," Emy's voice echoed in the wagon.

We all turned and looked at her. When did she show up into the wagon? We never even heard her come inside. It took a moment for the shock to wash over me. I shook my head.

"No, Emy. We cannot let you do this either." I ran over to her.

"We have no other choice, Sarah. This is how it must be." Samie gently placed her hand upon my shoulder. My heart sank. "So I am to lose yet another sister? Is this how it has to be played?" I turned my head to each of them. I shook my head. "I do not like this. Not one bit," I said, making it very clear to them.

"We will let them do their thing for the time being and we will prepare for the punch. You know that if he cannot have Samie, he will surely go for me first to get to her," Emy said.

"As long as things go as planned, we will have everyone else ready for departure out of here for safety. This way we can have a chance to regroup and evaluate what went wrong," Lor added to the overall plan.

I went and sunk back into the pillows. "But what if it doesn't work? What then?" I asked hopelessly.

This was suicide. I did not like it one bit. But, as always, the decision was not mine to make. They all joined me on the pillows. We just laid there in silence, comforting each other in the solitude. Emy joined me on my right hugging me. Lor on my left stroked my hair and Samie with her head upon my lap. We were all lost in our own thoughts.

Finally, I broke the silence. "But what if it does not work?" I whispered.

"At least you two will be safe," was all Emy said.

I squeezed her arm tighter against me as the tears welled up in my eyes. "I still do not like this plan. There must be another way. There has to be." I pushed back the tears, but it was to no avail.

"I do not see any other way as of yet. So this is to be the way. This is to be our fate," Emy added.

"I am sorry," Samie whispered.

"Why are you sorry?" Lor asked her.

"Because I thought of it," Samie confessed.

"This is not your fault, Samie. We would have thought of this either way," Lor reassured her.

She thought a moment on that. "I guess you are right," Samie agreed.

"He will not be as strong as he could be if we were to let Samie do this. I am strong but I feel that Samie is just that much stronger. With me, he will still need more to complete himself. With Samie, I fear she would be all that he would need," Emy said, explaining her plan. "He does want me. And since we will not let him have Samie, then maybe he will settle for me instead. That will give the rest of you a chance to get to safety provided I can get this to work."

I sighed deeply. "It will have to work, Emy. We have nothing else to choose from. This is our only hope. I do hope you are right about this."

We continued to lay there together for the rest of the time. We never even bothered to look through anything at that point. We wanted to stay there as long as we could before we gave up Emy to Orthus for good.

After some time, there was a soft knock on the wagon door. James and Aaron poked their heads inside.

"How are we doing with the research?" Aaron asked.

We sat up, startled slightly.

"I think that we have done enough for one day." Emy jumped up off of the pillows and over to Aaron.

'Not a word of this outside of us four,' I heard her thought in my head. We all nodded.

James and Aaron were safer not knowing what we knew. It was true. If Orthus went for Emy instead of Samie right now, they were safer not knowing ahead of time. These two would insist on packing everyone up and getting out of here as quickly as possible.

James gave me a curious look questioning me if all was alright in those eyes. I tried to smile to reassure him all was fine.

'No, it's not alright. But you cannot tell me right now either,' He thought to me. I frowned and shook my head no.

'Not at this time. You are safer not knowing what we know right now,' I thought back to him.

'Fair enough, I guess that will have to do.'

It broke my heart that I could not tell even James about the plan. But, Emy was right. Even James could not know. The less outside the four of us to know the better it was. The more likely we can get the plan put through without incident.

We went back to the cottage. James and Aaron had gone into the village after tending to Samie's father and took care of everything else.

"It looks like they are holding her mother in the cell for now. They are planning to start everything in another day or two. I think Orthus wants to see if Samie will come out to save her mother or not. It must be part of a game for him. What does he want Samie for that he would take her mother as a bartering tool? 'Show yourself or I kill her'." Aaron explained what they discovered in the village today.

Samie placed her head in her arms upon the table. I rubbed her back.

"You cannot give in to him or all is lost," I whispered to her.

"Why do they have to die just so I can live? It is not fair," she sobbed.

"Because they love you and will protect you until the day they die. If they were so afraid for their own lives, they would have given you up by now. But by continually saying that it was just the two of them all along, they choose to protect you. They saw how evil he is and they must have known to keep you hidden from him for that reason." Lor came and sat beside Samie.

"We will get through this, Samie, I promise. All will not be in vain." I looked at Emy questioningly with the last part.

'Will it not?' I thought to her.

"As long as all goes according to the plan, all will be fine," she assured.

Aaron looked at Emy. "What plan, darling? What have we gotten into here?"

"We have found ourselves in the middle of a mass witch hunt darling. Orthus has decided to try and kill us all off since no one in our family wanted to marry into his. I feel that it is his form of revenge. We just need to lay low as much as possible for now," Emy answered casually.

"So you mean Cloe is not going to be his only victim in this family? By the Gods, woman! What has happened while I was away?! And do not be painting it all pretty for me! I am not a dumb little kid!" Aaron grew angry at the comment.

"Aaron, darling it was not us. We had nothing to do with any of this. I refused to marry him. I found you. I married you. He has somehow convinced Tabitha to start pointing fingers at people for witch craft. She started with Cloe. Now, he has discovered how important Samie here is with whatever 'plan' he has been brewing so we have taken her in to protect this poor, innocent girl —" Emy had gotten up and moved towards Aaron. She placed her hands on his shoulders. She worked her fingers throughout the muscles on his shoulders and neck.

"It's always another innocent," he said, this time more calmly. He seemed to be becoming sleepy. Emy continued to work her hands over his shoulders.

"You must be very tired from all this drama after such a long trip," she said softly.

Aaron agreed, "Long trip, yes, yes. So much drama..."

"Maybe you should go down for a rest? We may continue this discussion after you have rested more fully," Emy crooned.

Aaron nodded. "Yes, that sounds wonderful. I shall go for a rest. It has been a long day." Aaron stood up from his seat and walked from the room.

After Emy made sure Aaron was settled in the bed, we continued our discussion.

"That was a little edgy. Do you think he will be alright with all of this after his rest?" Lor asked.

Emy shook her head. "I am unsure. It is hard to say. He is definitely becoming agitated over all of this. That is certain. We will have to start leaving him out of all of this from now on." We all nodded in agreement.

"Samie, you need to remain smart about all that has been going on with your mother. Orthus wants you any way that he can. He is trying to get to you by going after your parents. He hopes that you will step forward to keep her from being burned. But, if they have already set sights to try her, they will not stop even after they get you. She would still burn even after they got you," Emy continued.

Samie frowned but nodded that she understood.

"Sarah, why don't we start on those wedding plans? We can probably distract the villagers with a wedding to buy some time for Samie's mother. And with Nicolas' help, we can maybe sneak her in to see her mother, even if it is for a short time."

Samie smiled slightly. It may not be saving her completely, but at least it was something. A chance to see her mother meant the world to her right now.

"I was thinking that with everything that has been happening, we would just hold a private one here. Just for us," I started to say.

"That's fine." Emy smiled. "But, we also need to keep suspicions far from the family at the same time. We will need a church service as well. We can set it up for the next day? Or, we could hold ours much later on that same night?"

I understood. There is to be nothing private about this family from here on out. The villagers, and the church especially, would need to be included in every little detail of our life or they may pick one of us next– even though Emy offered herself as bait. We still need to try and keep them out of the house.

We cannot ever let them have a reason to look within these walls. Orthus may have our book, but we started a newer and better one. What he did not know is that most of what we knew was never written down within those other pages. It was all learnt when we were small. So we never had to write it down. But, now that we have started taking in others, we needed to write what we already knew down so the future generations would know what NOT to do. The last thing we needed was Orthus to get a hold of that one. If he was able to open it, we would all be in trouble.

The bigger question was how we were going to make sure no one else but Emy was singled out for the next time, once we were ready for it. We decided we would pay a visit to the minster in the morning to go over the church to go over the church services.

We would have the church service for the village during the day. But, then we would hold a more private setting here at the homestead in the gardens with the family that same evening. That seemed the easiest and the safest way to do things. This way, we could do the hand fasting as well, and no one in the village would be the wiser.

We decided to part for bed so that we may get an early start in the morning. Samie would stay with Lor and see if there were any spells to help pull Orthus with us when he tried to grab Emy. James and I would meet with the minister. This way, Emy and Aaron could deal with other things. Emy wanted to see what other information she could get out of the villagers and see if Nicolas could get us into see Samie's mother. So we said our good nights and headed to our beds.

Once we were in our bed, Samie whispered," Why do you not want me to be the one to try and take Orthus? Am I not strong enough to do so?"

I shook my head. "It is not that, dear. We are more afraid that if all goes wrong, not only would we lose you, but then he will be so strong we will have no hope in ever stopping him. You are plenty strong and capable of doing so. But, we do not want to give him the chance to get you."

She thought on that for a moment. Then, she asked," Why did you tell him that I belong to you and that he could not have me?"

I shrugged. "I guess since we took you from your home, you are under my care now. Almost like I am your foster mother?" I looked at her in my own uncertainty.

"So I have more than one mother now? My real one, but now, you as well, because of what has been happening?" Samie asked.

I nodded. "I...are you alright with that?"

She hugged me tightly. "Most definitely!" She snuggled close to me and fell asleep.

I smiled and closed my eyes as well. *I just hope I can keep you alive this time around,* I thought solemnly.

During the night, I saw Samie's mother in the cell.

"I'll watch the prisoner for now," Orthus said to Nicolas. Nicolas looked at his father suspiciously.

"What are you going to do to her?" he dared to challenge him.

"Oh, nothing that you need to be concerning yourself over. Go on now, off with you," Orthus responded smoothly.

Nicolas seemed very nervous about it. But, as his father willed, it was to be done. Nicolas left, but he stayed close by. He hid within the shadows just in case. His father wanted Samie bad enough to kill her father; there was no telling what he might do now with her mother. If he could touch her at all that is. He had grown remotely stronger after Cloe. But, that level of strength did not always last unless he was complete.

When Orthus thought that no one was around, he snuck into the cell.

"Hello, Martha. Do you remember me? Because I remember you. Oh most definitely, do I remember you," he said with a menacing smile.

She never even looked up. "Go away from here, Orthus. You were banished. How can you still walk here upon this earth?" she questioned.

Orthus laughed loud.

"Silly witch! As you were banishing me, I had Tabitha summoning me way over here!" He laughed again.

How she hated that laughter. It seemed to pierce right through your soul. "Remind me to thank her dearly for it." She stood up, smiling this time.

Orthus raised an eye brow. "Oh? And why are you going to thank her? Have you changed your mind?" He started to smile. He went to take her hands into his. His face brightened. "Have you decided to accept my proposal?"

It was her turn to laugh. "Do not be so silly." She looked deep into his eyes so that they pierced through him just like his laughter does to her.

His face changed. He looked puzzled.

She smirked and leaned forward towards him. She went to his cheek. "I get a second chance to kill you," she whispered and brushed a kiss upon his cheek.

Orthus went red. He slapped Martha across the face which made her fly to the ground. She landed on her knees and just sat there. She lifted her face towards him. Her brunette hair disheveled and covered her eyes partly.

"You witch! Do you really think I will let you kill me again?" he yelled at her.

She laughed crazily at him. "Fool that you are!" Martha returned.

"You will be burned at sunset!" Orthus proclaimed.

She bowed upon the ground at his feet, mocking him. "All hail! The great Orthus has spoken! So mote it be!" She laughed at him again.

He was getting furious with her now. "Why do you mock me, witch? I offered you everything! You refused me! And twice at that!" He pulled her up so they were nose to nose. "Why will you not be with me? You are not taken anymore," Orthus pleaded with her. "Were you not mine once? Why not now?" His eyes pleaded with her.

Martha hesitated for a moment. She never left his eyes. "Once, true we were each other's. But, that was only the once. Always and forever beside the Beltane fires, lost in time. But, do not forget what you did to me then, too," she whispered to him.

"What did I do to you, my dearest Martha?" he whispered back, his voice becoming soft and gentle once again, almost softer than I had ever heard from his cruel lips.

"You betrayed me, Orthus." She looked at him in sad awe.

Orthus looked as though he was slapped across the face. His eyes looked at her like a confused child. "How did I do that, dearest?"

"You forgot," was all that she said. She turned away from him. She did not want him to see the pain behind her strong eyes. *Did he truly not remember?* she thought.

Orthus looked at her. He shook his head. *What did I forget?* he asked himself. Memories ran through his head. He saw Martha's face as she smiled in the sun. The two of them laughed together. Then the pain when he had to leave the island. He was never to return there; never to return to her. He became a lost soul cast upon the world searching for a way back to the druids. But, he had done wrong and was cast out, forever.

"I am truly sorry. I had no choice but to leave so that you could stay. It was not my choice in the matter." He thought about his words and about their time together.

She shook her head. "I know *why* you left. This is not why I am mad." She turned to him. She closed her eyes and opened her arms. She had a faint glow around her.

"I showed you something once. But, you ignored it. You never came when I needed you. I will show you again." Flashes of the past appeared slowly. Martha grew younger. Her hair was long and flowing once again. Flowers were woven throughout it. Slowly turning to her side, she showed the round belly of being with child. Then, the belly disappeared. A pair of big brown eyes of a tiny toddler glowed brightly back at him. He watched all of this in awe and wonder. He shook his head. He flashed to Samie from the village.

"Samie? Ours?" he questioned. He whispered it upon the air. He stared in disbelief. "I have a daughter?"

Martha knelt down in front of him. She brushed his cheek with the back of her hand. "She must never know. Kill me if you must, but do not touch her ever. This is my dying wish. You will at least honor that. Will you not?" she begged him.

He stared back at Martha. "Why did you not send word another way? I could have sent for you," he babbled. *'Maybe I could have been different,'* he thought.

She shook her head and smiled sadly. "You would not have lasted. I saw into your heart. Sadly, you could not handle it. We both would have been gone long ago if we did try."

His eyes narrowed at that. "I would have tried for you! Was our love not worth fighting for?"

"Not when it is doomed to fail in this lifetime, Orthus. Any other lifetime, yes, we will stand side by side, arm in arm with swords swinging against the world. But, you have to stand alone while I protect her." She kissed his forehead and bade him to leave her be in her thoughts.

He left more distraught than he had ever felt in his life. His daughter. THEIR daughter. And he tried to kill her. He felt ashamed for not knowing this. Why did he not try to understand that dream years ago? Why did he push it away as just a wishful dream and not her actually being there, trying to contact him? How stupid he was! Has he lost his druid ways? Forgotten the teachings they had spent years learning? He retained most of them. Was she right? Is his heart really so black that there is no hope of him ever changing?

I left him to his thoughts. I opened my eyes in the dark. Samie was sleeping peacefully. I brushed her hair with my fingers. Poor child. She was to never know any of this. Not unless she finds out herself. Her "father" was murdered and now she was unknowingly planning to vanquish her real father. I would have to keep this from her for a little while. But, she would need to know eventually. If she was to ever find out that I knew this and never told her, she would hate me. I would lose her trust. I could not risk that trust disappearing. Protecting her relied on her trusting me. I would keep this secret for now. There will be a time and a place for it. Right now was not the time. I snuggled back upon the pillow and tried to go back to sleep.

In the morning, Emy and I took Samie and snuck into the village. Samie and I waited along the woods so no one else would see her.

"I will go talk with Nicolas," Emy said. We both nodded to her. We sat and waited for her return.

"How long do you think it will be before they decide what to do with my mother?" Samie asked.

I shook my head. "I am not sure on that. It all depends on if they can find anything to make hard proof that she must be a witch."

Samie frowned. "This is all to protect me, but it feels so wrong. Why can't we just take her out and run away?"

"It is not as simple as that. I am truly sorry. But, if we help your mother escape and we all go missing as well, they will search for all of us. Even if we get away now, who is to say that someone later on down the road will not travel to where we happen to be and recognize us? Then, we will all be in grave danger."

She nodded in understanding. "I see your point. Too bad it was not the case. Then, none of us would ever be in danger again."

I giggled. "That would definitely be a perfect world. I wish one existed." I looked over and saw Emy returning. We stood up to wait for her.

"After lunch Nicolas can sneak us in," Emy said.

After lunch, we met Nicolas outside of the cell.

"I can give you limited time. After Orthus being here last night, I do not think he will be coming again today." Nicolas said in hushed tones.

"What do you mean?" Emy questioned.

"He visited Martha last night," I informed her.

Nicolas looked shocked that I knew this.

"I was dreaming, sorry. It was highly interesting," I babbled.

Emy shook her head. "Let us be going." She pulled us inside.

"Momma!" Samie burst inside.

Martha turned, shocked and scared. Emy put her hand up. "It is alright. Nicolas snuck us in to visit with you. No one else knows about Samie."

Relief washed over Martha's face. She embraced her daughter with tears in her eyes.

"They still do not know about her. We have been keeping her with us."

"Thank you," Martha whispered.

"Someone killed Papa," Samie told Martha.

Martha looked up at us. "Orthus."

Emy and I looked at each other. Then, we looked at her.

"You know Orthus?" I asked even though I already knew.

"Yes. You could say we grew up together," Martha confessed.

'But, that is all *I will say here in front of Samie.*' She looked pleadingly at us.

Emy nodded.

I took Samie towards the door so Nicolas could watch her. "Stay with Nicolas. We just need to brief your mother about what is going to happen soon."

She nodded her understanding.

I pointed my finger at her. "Do not be listening, IN NO MANNER," I stressed.

She looked at her feet. "Yes ma 'am."

I went back inside and nodded to Emy. Emy was already telling Martha what we knew as of now.

I could not wait any longer. "Will you ever tell Samie the truth?"

Martha looked at me, confused.

"I know about Orthus. I saw it in my sleep last night. He came to visit you here."

Martha's heart sank.

I sat down next to her. "She needs to know. If he is her father, she needs to know that we are trying to vanquish him."

"I wish she did not need to know." Martha shook her head.

"Wait a moment. Orthus is Samie's father? Does HE know this?" Emy asked, shocked.

Martha's head sank lower.

"He knows as of last night. And, she swore him to secrecy," I answered, rubbing Martha's back to comfort her.

Emy started pacing back and forth. "So he never knew until just now? All of these years?"

"No. I kept it a secret from him all of these years. I knew his heart was too dark to handle such a love. He would have destroyed us both." Martha stared off into a void.

"After we do what is needed to be done, we will be moving away from this place. Samie will be coming with us. We will watch over her for you." Emy tried to ease Martha's mind on that a little. "This way the village will never know that she really does exist."

Martha looked at us. "What are you planning to do?"

"Actually, Samie helped think of it. One of us will be sacrificing ourselves to do this though." I paused. I looked at Emy sadly. She shook her head.

'I am not changing my mind. What's done is done,' she thought.

I frowned.

"As we are leaving our physical form, Orthus tries to go in and 'absorb' the life essence. That is how he retains his power to be as strong as he is. But, the one who goes will try to take him into the void with her instead of him taking her. We just need to make sure there is no spell or anything else that we need to do first beforehand."

"My Samie thought of that?" Martha asked, surprised.

We both nodded. "She is very bright. We have enjoyed her staying with us."

The door opened slightly. Nicolas poked his head in. "Time to be gone," he whispered.

We all stood up.

"Hold off as long as you can with telling her. Tell her only if you must. But, not as of yet. Samie should have a book buried deep within her trunk. She knows not of it. I placed it there for her. It may come in handy." Martha instructed as she hugged us good-bye.

We hurried out of the cell and grabbed Samie's hand. We ducked into the woods to walk back home.

"What did you discuss with my mother?" Samie broke the silence.

I glanced at Emy. *'What do we say?'*

'I'll handle this,' Emy thought.

"Handle what?" Samie asked. We both stopped in our tracks. Samie hung her head low. "Crap, I'm sorry. I can't help it, sometimes," Samie confessed.

"You must be more careful, child. This gift will get you into serious trouble if you are not. Around us is one thing. But, anyone else not close to the family, well, you see what is happening in this village? First Cloe, and now your mother. You best be having a better handle on this before we move. Else you will not be able to leave the homestead ever for everyone's safety," Emy scolded her.

"I said I was sorry," Samie whined.

I rolled my eyes. "It is not about being sorry, Samie. It is about being safe, and being smart about what you do. Your mother is going to the fire to protect you. Unfortunately, we are still not sure why Orthus wanted you so much. But, we think he may abide by your mother's last request and stay away from you," I tried to explain to her and somewhat change the topic, slightly.

"My mother spoke with Orthus? When was this?" Samie demanded.

"Last night. He went to see if she would give you up to 'save her life'. And she refused to. But, since the two of them have a history together, she requested that he stay away from you and leave you alone," Emy jumped in.

"History together? What kind of history together?" Samie started to get upset more.

'Now you've gone and done it,' I thought.

"Gone and done what?" Samie turned to me. "What are you not telling me?"

"Samie, firstly, stay out of my head. That will get you nowhere fast with me. I told you that before." I looked at Emy and shook my head. "We cannot possibly live like this."

"Fine," she said. She took Samie's shoulders and sat her down. "You need to sit for this one, sweet one." Emy took in a deep breath and closed her eyes for a moment. Samie looked up at Emy, waiting for what was to come. Unknowing to what awaited her one Emy breathed the words to her. I waited, too. More for Samie's reaction because I knew what was to come.

"Samie, the man that was killed was your father as you grew up, yes. But, he was not your *real* father. Do you understand me so far?" She looked at Samie.

Samie nodded. "I loved him and he is my father."

"I understand. He *raised* you. But, your *real* father did not ever know that you even existed until last night when your mother told him."

Samie started to shake her head. "You are lying. I will not listen to this further." Samie started to stand up. Emy pushed her shoulders down, making her plop back on the ground.

"You will stay and you will hear just what you were pressing into our heads to hear from our thoughts. There will be no more going into our heads. Is that clear, young lady?" Emy commanded.

"No! It is NOT CLEAR! NONE of this makes any sense anymore!" Samie started to scream at her.

"Samantha Jane! You will stop this at once," Orthus bellowed from behind us.

We all turned to look at him, shocked and scared both. He turned towards Emy, waved his hands, and said, "I mean you no harm, just this one and only time. I have been trying to wrap my head around this one all night."

Something clicked inside Samie's head. She jumped up and screamed, "NO! It cannot be!"

Orthus walked slowly to Samie. He wrapped her in a hug. "I am sorry about all of this. They are correct. I never knew. Your mother did it to protect all of you. And now, I will leave you in the care of your new mothers." He stepped back from the crying child and kissed her upon her third eye. "They can protect you from the likes of me better than I can myself."

Then, he bowed to us, said, "Good day, Ladies," and disappeared back into the woods.

Samie fell to her knees, sobbing. "This cannot be true. It just cannot! How can it be? The one we must be rid of is my own family?" She sobbed in her hands.

We both knelt beside her. We did not know what to say to her about this. We just sat there with her. Finally, she whispered, "Why have the Fates thrust this upon me? Why do they feel that I can handle this? Such a family tragedy." She shook her head. Samie looked at us and stood up slowly. "We might as well get going with this. The sooner it is over with, the sooner I can move on." She started to walk back to the homestead.

"Are you sure about this?" I asked her.

"Yes. If my own father feels that he is a danger to me, then I must protect not only myself, but all of those around me as well. If he is not stopped, then we are all doomed." Samie stared straight ahead. "I consider everyone in my family gone at this point. They will decide the death sentence for my mother. There is no doubt about that. They never see them innocent. They hunt and hunt until they find some hard 'proof' that will give them the go ahead on it. Even if it takes years."

We all walked silently back to the homestead. When we finally got back, we went on to different things. Emy went into the kitchen, I went to the gardens, and Samie went to Lor's wagon to look through the books. She said she needed to look for something.

Emy and I decided the church could wait until tomorrow. We had a boat load to swallow from today's events. Samie took it better than I had hoped. But, it was still hard to grasp the idea of Orthus being her father and that his own child was destined to destroy him, or be destroyed by him herself.

"A penny for your thoughts, lady?" I heard a voice behind me. I jumped a little and turned. James stood there smiling.

I smiled back at him.

"Having a rough morning?" He hugged me and kissed my forehead.

"Try rough week." I hugged him back and closed my eyes, savoring the moment.

"So I gathered. You have been picking from the same plant for twenty minutes now. And from what I see, there is not anything to be had from it." He smiled at me and guided me to a seat within the garden. "What is troubling you?"

When we got to Lor's wagon, I put my hand on the door handle and stopped. The handle seemed oddly warm. I looked at James. "Something is not right," I whispered to him. He looked puzzled. I motioned to him how the handle was warm. He felt it too. He peeked around the corners of the wagon, and then he motioned for me to move. He went inside first. Smoke billowed out of the wagon. James came out with Samie unconscious in his arms. Lor was somewhat conscious and staggering behind him. She coughed a little, waving the smoke away.

I ran towards Samie.

"Samie!" I exclaimed.

Lor put her hand on my shoulder. "She will be fine. It's just a spell that backfired, that is all," she explained.

I looked at Lor. "What do you *mean*, a backfire? Who was performing?" I asked.

"Samie was. She wanted to test a few things out. This one was supposed to make us 'poof' elsewhere. Needless to say, it did not work," Lor explained further.

I got so mad inside.

"She has to learn sometime, Sarah. At least I was here with her," Lor said.

James reemerged with a blanket and some smelling salts. We covered Samie with the blanket. I put her head on my lap while Lor waved the salts in front of her nose. It was taking too long with the salts.

"She's not coming to, Lor." I started to get anxious. "Why is she not coming to?" I checked her nose and mouth for air. She was still breathing. That was good. I moved from under her head. I had Lor hold her and I rubbed her hands.

"Samie," I whispered, trying to remain as calm as possible. "Samie, come back this way to me," I continued, slightly louder. I kept looking at Samie for any sign of her return.

"James, go and fetch Emy now, please," I requested, never taking my eyes from the girl. "Come on, Samie. I need you here. Where did you go?"

'Why did you do this to me?' I thought to myself.

'I just wanted to help,' I heard Samie inside my head.

Progress! She was still in there!

'Samie, sweetie! Where are you?' I continued in thought. If I couldn't guide her verbally, maybe I could do so mentally! It was worth a try.

'I am not sure where I went. I seem to have lost my way back, if that makes any sense,' I heard her, say, softly.

I closed my eyes. Focus, Sarah! What can I do to guide her? *'Can you feel my hands on your hands, love?'* I thought.

'No,' she responded sadly.

'Try, Samie. Imagine what it feels like. Focus child,' I urged her.

After a time, I stated to feel a tingle within her fingers. *'That's it! You're doing great, Samie! Keep going!'* I encouraged her on. She was slowly coming back.

I opened my eyes and looked at Lor. I nodded to her to wave the salts again.

'I smell something,' Samie thought to me.

I stared at her. *'Go to that smell. Open your eyes and see what it is, child,'* I told her.

Her eyes flickered slightly but remained closer still. *'I am scared to.'*

'Do not be afraid. Not all that is unseen is to be afraid of. Open your eyes and see the smell. Trust me,' I thought to her.

Her eyes flickered more and finally I saw those deep browns.

"I will never steer you wrong child." I smiled and hugged her tightly. "You are safe here," I whispered in her ear.

"I was so scared, Sarah. I didn't know where I went or how to get back. I, I," Samie whispered back to me. She sobbed.

I hugged her tighter. "It shall be alright, dear child. You are back now. Sarah has gotten you back home, love," I soothed her.

"I'm sorry." She sobbed more. "I seemed to have been following something and gotten lost."

I pulled away slightly out of the hug. I parted some of her hair from her eyes. I looked worriedly into her eyes. "What do you mean, child?" I asked her, growing concerned now. Maybe someone wanted her to find this meditative state and try it. Maybe they were waiting to distract her and take her that way. What could have happened if James and I did not get her when we did? So many thoughts ran through my head. That was much too close to becoming a tragedy for us. If she was any deeper in that state, there may not have been any saving her.

"Do you remember anything while you were in your trance? It may help me to figure out where you went to. Or, we can wait until later, if you would prefer?" I asked her.

"Yes, waiting a little may be better right now. I need to regroup myself, I think," Samie replied, still out of sorts.

I let her sit there for a time. Emy and James came running up the way. Emy knelt beside me next to Samie.

"What happened?"

"Samie wanted to try a spell that was supposed to 'poof' us from one place to another. But, it did not exactly do that," Lor answered with her head down.

"What did happen?" Emy questioned.

"We are not sure as of yet," I started. "Lor stayed. But, Samie here, went into a trance, it seems. She was physically here. But, her spirit travelled elsewhere."

I could see Emy go furious within. "Is she fully back now?" she said while she held back the building anger from what was just told to her.

"It would appear so. I managed to guide her back to us." I tried to ease her anger. "James and I got here and the door to the wagon was warm. James went in and helped get them out. There was smoke inside."

Emy sprung up from the ground. "What do you mean, smoke?"

I jumped back, startled. "Just what I said, Em, there was smoke." I looked at her, scared now. "There was smoke within the wagon when we arrived."

She turned towards James. She seemed so scared now. "Was there a fire inside at all when you got inside?" She had gone into his face, inches from his nose.

James stared at her and only nodded no.

She shot over to Lor next. "Did you have a fire going?" It was Lor's turn to be scared of Emy now.

"Is there something the matter, Emy?" I started towards her, trying to remain calm. She was making everyone on edge and alarmed now.

"Quite possibly, no. I mean, I do not know for sure. I cannot say anything, yet. I...I..." She paused and started to turn around in a small circle. She closed her eyes and continued to spin. We all just watched her.

'What in the world is this all about?' I thought to Lor.

She looked my way and shrugged. *'Beats me,'* she responded.

James stood by me ready to jump if Emy fell. Emy stopped after a moment. No one said anything. We just waited for Emy. Finally, she opened her eyes and looked at us.

"Someone coaxed you to try that spell, Samie. I would advise you to not try any more unless I am with you. It was poor judgment with the current circumstances to be trying anything on your own. Something worse could have occurred if James and Sarah did not arrive when they did. Promise me you will not do such a thing again."

Samie just looked up at Emy from where she still sat upon the ground. Emy glared down at Samie in concern. "Promise me, Samantha!" she bellowed at the child.

That jolted Samie back to us. "I promise," she whispered to Emy.

"Stay with Samie while I take a look inside." Emy directed. I nodded my understanding. Emy turned on her heel and proceeded into the wagon for further investigation.

It seemed like forever before Emy emerged from the wagon. "Lor, I would like you to have the wagon moved closer to the cottage. I do not trust it is safe here any longer," Emy said.

"Let us all go back to the cabin now and try to sort this episode out," Emy said as she walked past us without stopping. She headed straight for the cabin and away from the wagon quickly.

"Did you find anything of use, Emy?" I started to ask her. But, she was already gone to the cabin.

We all looked at each other. "I guess it is not to be discussed outside in the open?" Lor suggested.

I grinned and nodded. "I guess not." I turned to James and said, "Would you mind finding a suitable spot for the wagon?"

"Not a problem. You go on to the cabin and see what has her so spooked." James kissed my forehead and headed to the front of the wagon. He turned to Lor on the way, "Is there a special spot you would prefer, Lady?" He tilted his hat her way.

Lor gave a chuckle. "Anywhere that has a nice view, my dear soon to be cousin." She curtsied to him.

"I think that I may just have the perfect spot for you then." He gave a wink and hopped up in the wagon. Lor and I helped Samie to her feet and made our way to the cabin.

"What do you suppose has her all spooked like that? She has never acted like this before, has she?"

I shook my head. "Not that I can recall. But, I have a feeling it has to do with everything that has happened recently. Maybe Tabitha is trying to get at us in some way?" I thought about it.

"She is right to be mad at me. I should have waited to do that with her. I was not ready for such a feat," Samie said sadly. We stopped and looked at her. I almost forgot that she was here while I was lost in my thoughts.

I hugged her. "Oh, Samie! We have all done things where she has scolded us at one point or another! Do not fret your little head about that! She shall not remain mad at you over this for long. I promise," I assured her.

Samie shook her brown hair. "I hope you are right about this time. I am not so sure myself."

We walked on in silence the rest of the way.

When we reached the cabin, a wagon was outside. We all looked at each other. "Who do you suppose that belongs to?" Lor asked tentatively.

"I have a strange feeling that belongs to our beloved Tabitha," I said staring at it. I paused. "We need to hide Samie. If it is in fact Tabitha, she must never find out that Samie is real," I blurted.

Samie stopped dead in her tracks. "Was she the one there that night?" she whispered, scared.

I nodded to her. "She has been convinced by them to start these hunts. She is their pawn in their cruel game. You will not be safe until she leaves. As long as she has no knowledge of you, all will be safer," I explained.

"Come, James has gotten here with my wagon. We can hide you within there. As long as you promise not to try anymore spells while we are gone," Lor suggested and winked at Samie with a smirk.

Samie let out a chuckle. "Of course I will not do such a thing! I think I have learnt my lesson on that one!"

Lor grabbed Samie's hand and led her to the wagon to hide her.

"Wait for me before entering!" she called behind them.

I went closer to the cabin. But enough to remain out of sight from anyone by the windows. After some moments, Lor came running up. "Ready?" I asked.

She nodded. As we entered through the door, we put our minds blank in case Tabitha tried to enter our thoughts. We heard voices in the kitchen. We entered slowly.

Tabitha saw us and beamed. "Why, hello, Lor! It is good to see you again!" She rose from her seat and proceeded towards Lor to greet her.

Lor put up a façade. "Why, hello dear cousin! How have you been keeping? Staying out of trouble, I pray?" She stepped back from their hug.

Tabitha's face changed suddenly. She glared at me standing behind Lor.

"So you have been here long enough to hear of my escapades of late?" She smiled sweetly at Lor.

"Oh yes. I have been here for a few days now. I have been trying to get everyone situated in the group. A few of us needed medicinal supplies. So we have been tending the gardens and nearby forest for things to be restocked before we continue on our way again," Lor offered.

Perfect! I thought to myself. *If we keep to that pretense, things should go smoothly with her*

"Sarah! I almost did not see you standing there! How good it is to see you as well." Tabitha turned her attention towards me now.

Damn! When will I learn to not think around her? Damn, damn, damn, I thought. I threw on a bright big smile at my cousin. "Good day, dearest cousin! How goes the day for you?" I faked my kindness towards her as best as I could.

"Good. But I hear in the village that you are going to be married soon. I have to say that I am greatly saddened that you have not included me in this notification with the rest of the kinfolk. I had to hear tell of it from others in the village. Why, I was highly embarrassed to say the least of my not knowing."

So this is why you are really here, to see what more trouble you can cause upon your family, I thought silently. Anger welled up within me.

"Why, with all the fuss that has been going on, it must have slipped my mind, cousin. How terrible I feel about this all now," I replied as heartfelt as I could my eyes all the while glaring at her. I mustered a sweet smile for her.

"Oh, dearest! Do not be so sad about it. I can see you have gotten caught up with everything. I forgive you." She hugged me.

'You will not get any more than that out of me, Tabitha. I am not your pawn,' I thought out to her as we hugged.

She jerked away from me as though I had smacked her in the face.

'I don't use anyone as a pawn. I don't know what you are talking about.' Tabitha thought back to me.

I had to laugh through my anger. "Oh come now. Do you *really* believe you can fool those of us here with this façade? What are you really here for? Come now, out with it girl!" I shot at her.

She put her hand up and gasped in fake shock. "Why I do not know what you are talking about, cousin. I told you my business here today."

"Not all of it. I see right through your façade even if no one else can. Do you think we are all fooled by this? You had Cloe killed. Do you honestly believe we will allow you to partake in my wedding? Now what are you really here for?" I retorted, irritated at her by now.

Tabitha stood there staring at me. Emy started to make her way out of her seat. Tabitha glanced around the room.

"Where is the girl?" she finally blurted out, glaring at me now.

I raised my eyebrows and nodded. "Now see, was that so hard? Rather than beating around the bush by sweet talking us?" I asked calmly.

She kept glaring at me.

I smirked. "There is no girl here except what you see before you in this room. We do not have anyone else here to our knowledge. What girl do you speak of?"

Tabitha sized me up. I could feel her anger welling up within. "Martha's daughter, you fool. You know very well who I am after."

Now it was my turn to gasp in fake shock. "She had a daughter?"

Tabitha glared at me. She stepped closer to me. "You of all people here know damn well she did. Have you forgotten the day after Cloe? In the village when you stopped the villagers from attacking her? Accusing her of witch craft? I know *you* remember *that* much. You even convinced poor Nicolas to pull her away from the sight of the crowd when Emy distracted them for you." She tilted her head to one side to gauge my next reaction. She stood there, waiting for my next move.

I stood there, gathering my inner peace. *Keep cool, Sarah. Do not let her get to do what she always does.* I breathed deeply in, getting ready to respond.

Emy had already beaten me to it. She had flown Tabitha up against the wall by the neck. "What are you telling us, Tabitha?" she bellowed at her. "Was it you who started accusing the poor girl in the village that day? Was it not enough that we lost our sister, your cousin?! That you had to jump right into getting another burning up and running?" It was Emy's turn to glare at Tabitha.

Tabitha turned pale. She had forgotten that Emy was in the room. Tabitha was silent for a long time.

"Well? Out with it, woman! What was your plan? Who was that girl and why her?" Emy continued.

I stepped closer to the two against the wall and silently laid my hand upon Emy's arm. She glanced at me. I nodded for her to release her grip. Tabitha brushed herself off quickly.

"I believe Emy asked you a question, cousin," I said quietly.

Tabitha's head snapped towards me. She had a look of scared in her face because of what Emy just did. It had caught us all off guard. But, there was also a hint of relief in her eyes that I stepped in.

'*Do not stall too long, Tabitha. I may just leave the room and leave you to deal with Emy on your own,*' I thought to her. Her eyes widened with that. Now she knew that I was none too happy with her anymore as well. She pursed her lips tightly as though debating her next move.

"I am waiting," Emy sang.

Tabitha threw her hands up in the air. "Alright! Alright!" she replied finally.

We both looked at her, questioning the delay.

"Orthus said we needed her next. She was the key. That she was a strong one. She was stronger than even Cloe was. I was to get the crowd angered towards her so that there would have to be a trial for her next. He could sense her power," she blurted out. She looked at us pleadingly like a little child wanting a parent's approval.

"Did he know anything else about her? Did he mention anything else at all about this girl he is seeking?" Emy continued.

She thought about it for a moment. "Not that I can recall. He keeps a lot from me. I am on a need to know basis."

'*She is just a pawn to him, like we are to her. Let us be rid of her now,*' I thought to Emy.

Emy tilted her head to one side. "Not yet," she answered me, trancelike.

I raised my eyebrows at her. '*What else do you have for her?*' I questioned her silently.

Tabitha looked even more scared now, glancing at us back and forth.

"You shall see soon enough." She smiled.

Tabitha's eyes started to well up with tears. Her lower lip trembled with fear. "What are you planning to do to me, Emy? Remember, I am family," she muttered and pleaded.

Emy looked Tabitha over slowly. "Oh, and what was Cloe, then? Was she not family? Or was she just a rotten apple to be tossed aside into the compost pile? What about her?" I could see Emy getting mad at the idea.

"I, I," Tabitha stammered.

'Oh, Tabitha, what a mess you have woven for yourself now,' I thought to her, saddened.

Tabitha looked down at her feet. "I have nothing to say for that. I am nothing. I deserve whatever you do to me." She placed her head in her hands and began to weep softly.

"Yes, yes you do. Do unto others as you will have done to you threefold, Tabitha. What say you, girl? Should you be condemned to the fires like Cloe? Should we make you feel the flames slowly eating away at your flesh, while you scream, dying?" Emy suggested to her.

Tabitha grew silent at this thought. She took a deep breath and stood up straight. She lifted her head. "So mote it be. Do what must be done," she responded, looking Emy in the eyes.

'She's bluffing, Em! I do not believe that she is ready for death. Not this willingly. This is too easy of her agreeing to this,'

I thought at her. This was becoming too much. When was it going to end?

Emy smirked. "You are too easily agreeable to everything, Tabitha. Rest assured it will not be right now, little girl. Oh, no. You still have a role to be played out here, yet. You are nowhere near done. I will get you soon enough. Do not fret about that." Emy smiled brighter now. "Oh, no, my dear Tabitha. You still have to see this game of yours play out all the way until the end."

Tabitha's face went ghost white. It was clear now what Emy was planning. She was setting up the pretense for Tabitha to play our way now. We needed Emy set up and Tabitha was going to do it. Tabitha was going to be helping us defeat Orthus without even knowing it. Emy figured that if Tabitha thinks Emy is going to get her, she may just cause a trial against Emy to try and stop her before she does. Poor Tabitha, how easily she has now become our own pawn for our plan. Willingly become our pawn, too, and she doesn't even have a clue.

"For what it's worth, I am truly sorry about all of this, Em," Tabitha whispered.

"For what it's worth, Tabitha, it doesn't really matter anymore. What's done is done and all of the I'm sorrys in the world cannot change that now," Emy whispered back.

Tabitha nodded her understanding. Emy let her go. Emy stood straight and looked down upon Tabitha. "You are to leave this house and never enter here again. You are not welcomed in here any longer. Do not try to help with the wedding or meddle in any of our affairs in any way, shape or form. Is this understood, Tabitha?"

Tabitha nodded.

"You are no longer a part of this family. You have disgraced us with what you have done and will be doing so in the near future. I am sorrier to have to do this to you. Please leave now," Emy continued.

Tabitha looked up at Emy. She bowed her thanks for remaining to live and headed out the door. She looked behind her one last time before closing the door behind her.

I looked at Emy. She hadn't moved from her spot as Tabitha left. She just looked straight ahead, lost in her thoughts. I rested my hand on her shoulder. "Emy?" I whispered.

She continued to look forward. "The trap has been set. The bait has been taken. Now we wait and finish planning," was all Emy said. I nodded my understanding. It was what I had thought. She was setting Tabitha up to become our pawn in the trap to stop Orthus. By threatening Tabitha, the thought that she would be coming after her when she least expected it and of the possibility of her end being the same fate as that of Cloe's, Tabitha was sure to run to Orthus about this. They will plan now to go after Emy in hopes of stopping Emy from going after Tabitha. It was a sure fire way to get Emy into the position we needed her to be in. Unfortunately, I feared this was going to be sooner than we had hoped for. Emy is sealing her fate herself. She always needed to be calling the shots.

"Are you certain you wanted to do things like this, Em? Are we going to be ready for this in time?" I questioned her.

"I do not know at this time. But, it was as good a time to get the ball rolling as it will ever be. We need to act soon or they will go after someone else who does not have anything to do with this," Emy answered, uncertain herself if was a well thought out plan or not.

I looked at Emy for a moment and wondered if things would turn out alright at this point. "I best go check on Samie," I said and turned to go out of the room. I left Emy still looking straight ahead as Aaron got up from his seat to make sure she was alright.

I watched as Tabitha's horse trotted down the path and off towards the village. I didn't dare move until I was certain she was long out of sight. I looked across the land. Quiet as can be hoped for. I walked over to Lor's wagon where I hoped Samie was still within.

I knocked softly and opened the door. "Samie," I called softly. "Tis just me." I entered into the wagon and shut the door behind me. It seemed too quiet in here. "Samie, I'm back. Tabitha has left. I hope that she shall not be returning here anytime soon." I walked over to the cushions piled on one side. I was starting to get nervous. Where is she? Did Tabitha set us up to be distracted? Did someone else come in here and take Samie from me? Thoughts started to run rampant in my head.

Suddenly the cushions moved. Samie sat up from underneath them. I threw my hand to my chest in relief. "Thank goodness you are safe!" I spat out.

"Is everything alright?" she asked as I helped pull her out from under the pile.

"Not really. Tabitha is gone, which is good. But, I think Emy helped to jump start our little plan," I explained.

Samie looked at me and frowned. "How did she manage to do that?" We stumbled together as the cushions released her.

"Let's just say she threatened, well no, that is too harsh of a word. She *promised* Tabitha that she would have the same end of life as Cloe got and that she would see to it," I confessed.

Samie stopped dead. "She did not. Please, please, PLEASE tell me she did not tell her she would come after her," she blurted out.

It was my turn to frown. "I am afraid so."

"Damn it! Why would she do something so dumb?" Samie threw her hands up in the air in frustration. She started to pace the wagon.

"Because that's what she does. She has to be the one calling the shots. She has to be in control of the situation. It was convenient at the time to do so. Tabitha set up the pretense for it. She was pretending to be concerned about my wedding plans when she was really snooping for you. So Emy decided to make her our pawn for once. We are using Tabitha for our plan. She doesn't even have a clue we did this to her. Now she will run off to Orthus and try to get Emy before Emy can get her."

Samie stopped pacing for a moment. She tilted her head to the left and wrinkled her nose. She stood there contemplating what I had just said. After some time, she started to nod her head. "You know, that is really not so bad of an idea now that I think of it."

I looked at her in shock. "What are you talking about? We don't even have a full plan as to what we have to do when push comes to shove!" It was my turn to get frustrated now. "How can you see this as a good thing? What is so good about this?" I questioned.

Samie smiled sweetly. "It's brilliant, actually. Making Tabitha so scared straight that she does the job for you to get easier access to Orthus and get him into the position we need to get him. If it doesn't look like it was all Tabitha and Orthus' idea, they may be more hesitant to go for it like we need them to. Making Tabitha into our pawn for once instead of being used by her is brilliant."

Now it became clearer to me. Use the user to our advantage. She was right though. If it did not look more like Tabitha and Orthus thought of going after Emy on their own, they may not go after her at all.

"Let us be going into the house now. It looks like Tabitha is gone now," I said. So we walked back to the house. When we got inside, we could hear Aaron fighting with Emy.

"What did you say to Tabitha? And I mean the part that sent her running scared, Em. Do not be playing any games with me," Aaron demanded.

"Fine, I shall tell you. I told her never to show her face around here again or she'll end up like Cloe," she admitted.

Aaron threw his hands up in frustration. "Damn it, woman! You know she's going to tell this to Orthus. Are you *trying* to get yourself killed?"

Samie and I stopped in the doorway. I raised my hand to paused Samie from speaking. *'This is not our argument,'* I thought to her. She nodded.

Emy paused a moment. "Yes, actually. Well, kind of."

Aaron's eyes grew wide. "What are you trying to do?" he screamed at her. He crossed the room and grabbed both of her arms. "Why?"

"Because I must stop him and stop this madness that he has started. Or the whole village will be damned," she whispered.

"You have to stop him? Just you? It's always just you. No one else has to take on this responsibility of stopping this?" Aaron narrowed his eyes at her, trying to make sense of this.

"Yes. It has to be me. Samie is too strong to handle this yet. If it goes wrong, we will be far worse off. With me, he will still need more victims. I have to do this to save the village."

"What do you mean?" Aaron started to loosen his grip on her arms.

"You are better off not knowing too much."

He threw his arms up in the air. "Am I better off not knowing about how my *wife* is planning to have herself killed? Just to save the village? A village that has already willingly sided against her and her family to have her sister killed?" he rambled on in desperation.

She wrapped her arms around his neck and kissed his cheek. "Because that's who I am. It's what I do."

He sighed wearily. "I don't agree with it and I don't like it."

"I know. And you will never understand fully. But, that is why I love you so much; because you care about me so much." She hugged him tighter.

"Sometimes I wish I didn't. Then maybe it wouldn't bother me so much."

I took that as a cue to cut in. I did not need them in a full blown argument right now.

"Emy! We're back!" I called and reopened and shut the door so it did not seem like we had been standing there listening the whole time.

Emy turned in a whirl. They were both so caught up in their conversation they jumped at the sound of my voice. We stepped into the room.

"Oh, did I interrupt? I can leave you for now." I made to turn and leave the room.

"Actually, I was just going to go chop some more wood," Aaron said. He grabbed his hat and made for the door. Once he left, I went closer to Emy.

"Is everything alright? I mean with the two of you?"

Emy turned away from me. "Oh, yes. Perfectly fine, never better." I could tell that she was lying. I caught a glimpse of her dabbing the corner of her eye.

I wrinkled my nose. *'Are you sure?'* I thought to her.

She turned her head at me and said, "Yes."

I raised my hands, palms facing out, and said, "Alright."

Samie whisked by me and grabbed both of Emy's hands. "What an absolutely brilliant plan you just did! Sarah told me about what just happened when Tabitha was here. Brilliant!

~ 127 ~

Simply brilliant! I would have never thought of something like that! Ever!" Samie started to ramble on about how great she thought Emy's plan was.

Emy forced a smile upon her face. She was having second thoughts about what she did earlier after her conversation with Aaron. Samie was so clueless about it right now. Or at least she was acting like she was.

"Thank you, Samie, really." Emy forced a smile towards her.

"Samie, I think Emy needs a moment in her thoughts —"

"No, no she does not. She wants out of her thoughts. So, I am here to distract her from them so that they do not start to eat her up," Samie cut me off, explaining herself.

"No, Samie is right. I could use a distraction from my thoughts." She walked towards the far side of the room and glanced out of the window. She stood there for what seemed like forever. Then, she turned back towards us. "We have best get a step on this plan then. We mustn't delay any longer. Because of what I did today, we do not have much time left to work on this, I am afraid." She walked back to where we were and grabbed our hands. She guided us to the door. We walked like that all the way through the woods and to Cloe's resting place.

"Em, why are we here? Is everything alright?" I stammered. I was starting to get nervous coming back here. Also, she was silent the entire way.

She turned back almost as though she had forgotten that we were still with her. "Oh my! I am so sorry! I guess I must have gotten caught up in my own thoughts just then! Dear me! Yes,

yes. Everything will be just fine. I assure you, dearest sister. It will all turn out just fine," Emy rambled. She looked me in the eyes, and said, "I promise."

"Then why have we come here? What does this place have to tell us that we don't already know?" I took a half a step back. I was still uneasy about what Emy was up to suddenly. It did not seem like she was herself at the moment. That was making me the most uneasy.

Emy started to get excited about the place we were at suddenly.

"Who are you?" I blurted.

Emy stopped suddenly and looked at me. She had a questioning look on her face.

"You are not Emy within. You are not my sister. Who are you?" I repeated.

She let out a chuckle. She skipped around a few circles. "You were right, Deary! She caught on quickly to our little switch!" She laughed to the sky.

'It will be alright, Sarah. Trust me. And trust her. She knows what needs to be done. But we must be shown, not told how to do so,' I heard Emy's voice ring in my head.

'Are you certain of this? Will you be allowed to go back afterwards?' I thought back, hoping that this did not backfire on her.

'*Trust me,*' was all I heard in my head. The woman that was now within Emy circled around a few more times. "Oh it feels good to be young for a spell!" she sang.

I gave her an untrusting look as raised she her hands. "Truce. I mean you no harm. I wanted to show you something your sister Emy said you needed to learn. So we switched so I may show you that. Once you have acquired this then I will return to my body and Emy, to hers– I promise. I will not stay in her body forever. I am an old woman who has lived out her youth many, many moons ago. I have no desire to live forever like someone else that we know." She tried hard to convince me of this. I still kept my guard up for now. I could not take this chance no matter what.

"Let us give her a chance to prove herself. She seems worthy if Emy has agreed to this and go this far." Samie placed a hand on my shoulder to comfort me.

I looked at Samie. I wrinkled my nose at this notion. "I still don't feel right about this. Something could go wrong," I said, confessing my feelings about the whole situation.

"What do you need to teach us, wise one?" Samie started us off.

Emy's head nodded. "Right. Let us be getting on this. From what Emy has told me, you girls may not have a lot of time left to get prepared for this."

I nodded. At least she was right on that.

"Orthus is a tricky one to deal with and I am sorry that you got stuck with him. But what's done is done and cannot be undone. At least I know how to "trap" the likes of him as needed."

"So you have dealt with Orthus before?" Samie asked.

"Actually, it was his father I was able to get rid of. Orthus, was already sent away to learn how to be better. His mother sent him somewhere she had hoped he would be safe and others would be safe from him," she answered.

I looked at her. "His father? So it does go in the family," I blurted out loud.

"Yes, unfortunately, not all of them can stay away from this evil need to remain alive. It almost becomes an unhealthy obsession to have to beat the fates. To be one of them and control your length of life."

"Understood. We don't have much time, so we best be getting on this," I suggested.

"Rightly so, but remember, timing is Key for this. If you time this wrong, all is lost..."

We continued throughout the day, learning and practicing what she knew of the plan. She was right. Timing would be important when we finally went through with this. If we were too early or too late, things would be far worse than they are now. She taught us how to leave our bodies like her and Emy did.

After the day disappeared and the moon started to rise up high, she said her good-byes to us. "Goodbye, Lovies. I hope these lessons today will serve you well." She gave us each a hug.

"Wow, what a long day! Remind me not to get too old too quick!" Emy blurted out.

I narrowed my eyes. "Emy? Is that you?" I asked.

She smiled brightly at us. "Sure is! Did you learn enough for us to use?"

"I hope so."

"I think we can do this. With what we learnt today and what we already know, we should be able to do this."

"Good, let us be on to home. You can show me tomorrow what you learnt from her," Emy suggested.

We headed on home for the night. When we arrived, there was a wagon outside. We all looked at each other.

"I wonder who that belongs to," Samie said.

"Samie, you should probably go back to Lor's wagon until we know who this is."

"The girl who doesn't really exist will go hide in the wagon," Samie complained and turned towards the wagon.

I looked at Emy. "We need to stop trying to hide her like this."

Emy shrugged. "What do you want me to do? I cannot stop people from just showing up, you know. It's for her safety. She'll be fine. Once the plan goes under way, she will not need to be hidden any longer."

"Well of course not, because we will probably be in a new place after that," I retorted without thinking.

Emy stopped. Her eyes dropped to her feet. She twisted her mouth. "You're most likely right about that. The family will have to be moved because of this, especially if it works. But, as a safety precaution, I will want everything packed up and ready to go either way. Fail or succeed. We are on the move."

I felt sorry for the way I'd just spoken. Even sorrier about what Emy had just said. I couldn't think of any words right then. All I could do was hug Emy.

"We should get inside and see who our visitor is this time."

"Yes, we should."

So inside we went. When we stepped inside, we heard voices in the common room.

"I am sorry, Father. I really do not know where she is right now. But, I promise, we will both stop down to see you soon to make all of the arrangements that must be done." James was explaining to the visitor.

Of course! We needed to meet soon with Father St. Paul. But, why did he decide to come pay us a visit tonight? We looked at each other. Emy nodded. We all entered together.

"Good evening, gentlemen. I hope we did not keep you too long. Had I have known that you would be coming out to pay us a visit, Father, I could have made sure all of my evening chores were taken care of earlier." Emy tried to show her embarrassment of not knowing he was coming out to visit.

Father St. Paul stood up towards Emy. "It was no trouble, dear girl. I mainly wanted to congratulate the lucky couple." He smiled brightly. "It shows how we can still have good even among all of the bad. Love can still occur even during a loss of a dear family member." He took Emy's hands in his and patted them. "I am truly sorry for what they did to Cloe. She was always a sweet child. It is a shame that they did that to her."

Emy smiled. "Thank you so much, Father. It truly means a lot to me."

He offered his seat to her. "Please, sit. I can stay a while longer if you would like to speak more? I heard Tabitha rambling earlier this afternoon about her visit up here earlier in the day. I wanted to make sure all was right. Please." He gestured to the chair for Emy.

"Why thank you, Father. Maybe I will sit for a small time. I still have lots to do though. So I mustn't be too long." She tried to sound like she was still very busy with housework. I felt her unease when he spoke of Tabitha. Once Emy was seated, she asked curiously, "What did Tabitha have to say exactly?"

'Way to beat around the bush, Em,' I thought.

'Shh. The Father and I are always blunt to each other. We always have been,' Emy snapped back at me.

I wrinkled my nose and looked down at my feet in embarrassment.

"Surely, you can only imagine what she tried to get me and everyone else to believe." He let out a hearty chuckle.

Emy smiled shyly. "Yes, she does have a way of letting her imagination get the best of her at times, doesn't she? But come, I can imagine all sorts of things and none of it would be anywhere near the truth. What is she up to?" Emy shifted to the front of the seat.

Father St. Paul heaved heavily. "She is trying to say that you are out to kill her. She said that you promised that she will be dead in the same manner as Cloe. She is out right terrified Emy. What happened here today?" he said softly.

"Ah. I am afraid that I may have let my temper get the best of me today with that girl. You see, she came up here under the pretense of being hurt of us not telling her about Sarah and James' wedding coming up. After some prying, we found out she was really snooping around to see if we knew anything about a missing young girl. Martha's daughter she said," Emy calmly explained.

The father shook his head sadly. "We have discussed that temper of yours child. You must not let Tabitha get to you like that. Especially in the wake of what has been occurring of late. She will be out to get you next." He rubbed his hands along the top of his head, ruffling his short curls. "You might end up like Cloe yourself if you are not more careful," he whispered.

Emy stood up and put a hand on his shoulder. "What's done is done. That I cannot change. If it must be that fate for me, then so be it. It is what was destined for me all along. Do not fret over me any longer. Things will be fine, I promise." She tried to console him as best as she could.

"Emy, you make it so hard for your Godfather to keep his promise. I love you dearly, child. But, right now," he said.

~ 135 ~

"I am sorry, Godfather. But, this is something that must be done. I cannot tell you anything more about this. I am sorry that I let Tabitha get the better of me this time. Maybe I did let it go too far this time around. But, it will all work out in the end for the better, I promise you. But, Please, I beg you; do not question me further on this topic. You are best to not know the full story about this. Trust me. It is safer the less you truly know," Emy pleaded with him.

He sighed. He was silent for a few moments, gathering his thoughts. Then, he looked at her and said, "I only want to keep you safe. I promised your parents both that I would watch over you for as long as I was alive. If something wrong comes from today's altercations, I will not be able to forgive myself for breaking that promise. This is why it is so hard for me not to question your actions of late. Who is this girl she is looking for so badly? And why does she want her?" he pressed on.

She sighed and looked at me. *'You know it'll just kill him to not know. We have to tell him something. He is a good ally at this point in the game,'* I thought to her.

'But, at the same time, knowing may seal his death sooner as well. I am torn with this, Sarah. He has been there for everything,' she thought back at me.

"What if we treat it like the confessional?" I blurted out loud. "Then you are both protected."

James stepped towards me and placed his arms around my shoulders. "What a wonderful idea! Then they cannot use any information on the stand at any trial!" He looked at them.

Father St. Paul looked at Emy concerned. "Trial? What kind of trial? What is going on, Em? Does it have to do with what has been occurring presently?" His face was one of pure worry.

"Is this confessional?" Emy replied. *'This just might save all of us for a little while,'* she thought at me.

Father St. Paul put his hands in the air. "Yes, Yes! By my God, yes child this will be deemed confessional! Now, will you just tell me what is going on?"

"Very well." Emy smoothed a crease in her skirt. She lifted up the front of her skirts and knelt down in front of him. She made the sign of the cross. "Bless me Father, for I have sinned."

He put his eyes towards the heavens. *'Why does she do things so difficultly?'* I heard him think. I held back a giggle at that. He made the sign of the cross and started with the confessional process. He sat on the chair nearest to Emy. His voice went softer, calmer in this mode. "Now, what is troubling your soul, child?"

Her head stayed down and her hands folded in her lap. "The child Tabitha seeks is Martha's daughter. She does exist. We have her here in safety. Tabitha is doing Orthus' bidding. He wants her not Tabitha. Tabitha owes Orthus a debt that will never be paid, even in death. But, he wants her for reasons others will deem him as a devil or as Satan in the eyes of the church. He poses to be for the church. But, he is really not. He wants to do these witch trials so he may have women killed. He wants their essence of life so he may live longer. He seeks eternity. He feels the child in question is the key. The only problem is that the child is his own daughter reared by Martha. They both know this now.

~ 137 ~

"I had hoped he would not seek the child after learning this and per the dying wish of Martha herself. This seems to be the case not. He still seeks the child and we seek to keep her hidden and safe until we may be rid of Orthus once and for all. Otherwise, I fear no one will be safe ever from him. I must do what I did to make things happen, so that I may save the child. I am sorry for my sin. But, this is what must be." She kept her head down as she finished her spiel.

Father St. Paul just sat there in contemplation. He was trying to wrap his head around what Emy just told him. Hearing it like that made me realize just how complex our situation really had gotten. He rubbed his fingers along his boney chin.

"Aaron, James, I think we will need more logs on the fire. Would you both mind fetching more? I have a feeling this will be a long night."

I tilted my head in wonder. *'What do you suppose he is up to?'* I thought to Emy.

'I do not know for certain. But, I feel that he wants a word alone,' Emy thought back.

We waited for the men to leave.

"Now, what are you *really* trying to get at, Emy?" Father St. Paul finally pushed.

"Just what I told you, sir."

"You are holding something back from me, child. I just know you are. I am here to try and help you in any way that I can. Please, let me in," he begged.

"Emy, we should tell him. Maybe there is a way he can help," I finally spoke up. "If we have to do this, the more help the better, right?"

"I can tell there is more to this. But, you do not want Aaron to know. I understand this. I do. But, please do not leave me in the dark about this," he pleaded further.

"I can't tell you, I am sorry." Emy stood her ground.

'But Emy, maybe he can help us when we have to actually go through with this. We have to tell him.' I wanted to yell it at her.

She shot me a look. It always made me feel hopelessly out of control when she sent me that look. She wanted to not tell him no matter what.

I closed my eyes. *'Forgive me now, then!'* I thought at her. I knelt down where I stood, made the sign of the cross and babbled, "Bless me Father, for I have sinned."

'Sarah, what are you doing?' Emy interjected into my thoughts.

I kept my eyes closed and continued babbling. "What is being done, what has to be done, is that Emy must be tried as a witch so that Orthus can have her. We have to get Orthus in the act of getting Emy's essence of life so that we may counteract his spell. He pretends to be a part of the church. He has been heading up witch hunts everywhere he goes. We have seen a town where only the men folk are left. The town Orthus came from before coming here. He had set up a witch hunt and before they knew it, all of the women folk, little girls included, were tried and killed. We cannot allow Orthus to continue like this. We must stop him. We have to sacrifice ourselves for the safety of everyone else. This is what Emy does not want to tell you."

"Sarah!"

Father St. Paul stood there in shock. He looked from me to Emy. "Emy, is this really what is going on? Is Orthus really pretending? His papers seem like they are all in order. I do not understand this. They are papers from the Vatican." He sat down, staring straight ahead. "Could they be behind this? What could they possibly be up to?" He trailed off in contemplation. We all sat in silence for what seemed like eternity.

"So what can I do? I will help. I need to stop the church from continuing in this direction," Father St. Paul burst out suddenly.

We both snapped our heads up at the sound of his voice. We stared at him.

"No, this is too dangerous for you to get involved in. I cannot allow it," Emy said.

"No, the church has already brought me into this by bringing Orthus into the picture. I must fix what evil has entered my church. I must protect every creature here. I must protect every soul, including you two," he proclaimed. "It is my job to protect the souls of this community. If I keep losing those to this witch hunt, then I fail as a priest. I fail as a servant of The Lord."

Emy nodded in understanding. "I understand now. You have to help. You have no choice. But, I feel that the way our plan must go, I am to be lost to all in order to ensure Orthus' demise. I must do what must be done to help you protect these souls." She seemed awakened to this new addition of help now. "We may have a purpose for you after all." She smiled.

'Prayer' was all I heard in my head.

My eyes lit up. "Yes! That's it! Why, it is perfect!" I jumped up to my feet in excitement.

Father St. Paul looked confused with my newfound excitement.

I grabbed his hands. "You pray to protect Emy's soul while Orthus does his thingy! It just might be enough to help Emy to counteract what he is doing. This just might work! Orthus will not get Emy's soul! Not if we do this right," I babbled happily.

I looked at Emy. "Em, it just might be the extra kick that we need!"

"It just might work," Samie said quietly as she snuck into the room. We all jerked our heads in her direction.

"Is this the child they are all a fussing over?" Father St. Paul asked quietly as he walked over towards her.

Samie curtsied. "I am, sir. My name is Samie. I am Martha's daughter."

He looked her over. He took her head into his hands and kissed her forehead. "Bless you, child. I am sorry for all of this that has been put upon your family. You are strong through all of this thus far. And, I can see that you will continue to be strong through even more. Stay brave little one," he said to her.

He turned to Emy. "I will be in touch, soon. I will see how I can deter them for the time being if they do suggest anything right now. I will find something to counter Orthus that we can all use. I bid you all good night." He grabbed his hat and made for the door. James and Aaron were walking back in as he left.

"Leaving already, Father?" Aaron asked.

"Yes, yes. I forgot that I must be at Lady Hadlow's house in the morning. Emy was kind enough to offer me a tea for her ailment to try out. Good night gentlemen." He tilted his hat and left.

"Good night then, Father," they both answered.

Aaron looked at Emy. He raised his brow. "Is everything alright, love?"

She smiled sweetly. "Perfectly. All is well."

'Liar,' I thought at her.

'Silence for sure this time, Sarah! Silence!' she snapped back at me.

I put my hands up slightly to show peace. I would never dare say anything to Aaron. Not until it was absolutely necessary. And, it was not necessary to do so yet.

"Everything is fine for now, Aaron. There is nothing to worry about as of yet. Father St. Paul said he will help keep an eye and ear on Tabitha in case she says something she shouldn't be and remind her of something from her past. All should be fine," I tried to assure him for her.

'Better?' I thought at Emy.

'Yes, thank you.'

"We best be getting off to bed then. Come Samie. We will leave these two alone." I nudged Samie and James to the kitchen for privacy. As I turned to close the double doors to the parlor, I glanced at Emy. *'All is as it should be,'* she confided to me.

As I entered the kitchen, James bombarded me with questions. I held up my hand for him to silence and calm down. I walked calmly to the fireplace and picked up the already warmed water hanging above the fire. I poured three mugs of water and added some tea to each one.

I brought them over to the table and placed one in front of each of us. I sipped quietly for a moment. James made to start and stopped again about five times during this entire process. He was getting anxious and I knew that if I started too soon, things would explode in here. Once he seemed calm and started to finally drink his tea is when I started to speak.

"That was the beginning of a large storm that is coming. Emy saw her window of opportunity and took it by using Tabitha as her pawn for once. Father St. Paul came to make things right again and to try and prevent Tabitha from creating a huge scene than needs to be. We have now gained his help in our plan to be rid of Orthus once and for all. We have realized that we need all the help we can get, even though a select few need to remain in the dark still. I cannot tell you very much more than that right now. Do not breathe a word to Aaron about this in any way. Understood?" I paused for a moment to make sure he still followed me. James nodded. "What I can tell you is that once this plan really gets its wheels spinning, we will need to move away from this place, forever." I looked right into his eyes. "Are you alright with that?"

James placed his mug down. "I will go anywhere that you go, my love; even if it means to the ends of the world."

Relief washed over me with his response. "Good. Should we all turn in for the night and further this tomorrow when we may have Emy and Lor in on this?" Samie asked.

"It has been a long evening. Shall we?" I smirked at James.

He nodded. "Tomorrow it is, then."

Samie headed up the stairs. James grabbed my hand gently. "May I have a word, Sarah?" he asked softly.

I nodded. "I shall be up in a moment, Samie. Go on ahead, dear."

She nodded and continued on. I turned to James. "What's the matter?" I asked.

"Nothing is the matter. I wanted to give this to you earlier, but things got us all a little, distracted." He pulled out a small package wrapped in brown paper.

I smiled in surprise. "What is this for?"

"Oh, nothing much. I had seen it on our travels and thought it would suit you."

I carefully opened the package and pulled out a long thick chain. Attached to the chain was a mirror wrapped in gold. James gently placed it around my neck.

"It's lovely. Thank you." I kissed his cheek.

He smiled. "I should be going, now. We have a lot to do tomorrow."

"Oh! Yes, yes. See you in the morning, then." I was a little confused in my response. I thought he would have had more to say.

When I got into the bedroom, Samie began excitedly, "What did James want?" She jumped from the bed, beaming with an ear to ear grin on her face.

I smirked and raised my eyebrow. "He just wanted to give me this," and I held up the mirrored necklace towards her.

She laid the necklace in her hands. "Oh how lovely!"

"He really didn't have to," I responded.

"Of course he did. He saw something that reminded him of you. So he got it. It's meant for you."

"But he already gave me the ring. Is that not enough? I do not need a lot."

"Oh. I get it. Too many gifts, too close together." Samie nodded her understanding in the thought. She shrugged. "Maybe he felt that it would be useful to have it now?"

I wriggled my face and nodded. "Maybe that is it. With all that has transpired the last few days, who knows what will happen next anymore!"

Samie laughed. "THAT is for sure!" We chatted softly the rest of the time until we drifted to sleep.

When Samie and I got downstairs in the morning, Emy was already bustling around the kitchen. She must have been up for hours because there was barely anything for us to do to help. We looked at each other and shrugged.

"Good morning, Em!" I said cheerfully as we continued our way into the kitchen.

"Sit, sit, sit. Everything is almost ready," she said as she busily scurried around the room.

I sat quickly at my seat and motioned Samie to the same. Samie had a confused look on her face.

'What is up with Emy this morning? I do not like this behavior from her. It makes me nervous for her,' Samie poked into my thoughts.

'There is nothing to worry about. This will pass soon enough. She wants to hurry Aaron out of the house so we can have privacy with everything is all. A simple task it is.' I poked back at her. I smiled brightly so as to reassure her that all was well.

She gave me a hesitant smile back. "Are you certain?" she asked aloud.

"Positive. She has done this before. All is well. Sit." I gestured toward the chair again.

We sat at the table waiting until Emy was done. Finally, James, Aaron and Lor arrived in the kitchen. Aaron made his way towards Emy. James and Lor sat at the table.

Aaron had to catch Emy in his arms to stop her from darting to yet another task. He dipped her back and kissed her. "Good morning, beautiful. You have been up well before me this morning. Have you done everything by yourself today?" he asked after the kiss.

Emy adjusted her cap and smoothed out her skirt. "Why as a matter of fact, yes. I have. I have a busy day planned for Sarah and Samie and I wanted to be able to get to it right away after breakfast. I want no time wasted today. You will all hurry up in your meal and be off so I can get the added chores done quickly today," she ordered.

Aaron clicked his heels together and made to salute Emy. "Yes, my love!" he said with a giggle.

She smirked while she squinted her eyes at him. "Wise guy."

"That's why you love me!" He smirked back as he took his seat.

After the meal, James and Aaron made their way into town. They had to get the ship ready for the next sail. We looked at Emy after they left.

"So what's the plan now?" Samie asked.

"We harvest," Emy responded. The three of us looked at her puzzled.

"What do you mean?" I asked finally.

"Well, if Tabitha performs her role correctly, which I have no doubt that she will, I want the rest of you to move out afterwards." She raised her hand up towards me anticipating my protest. "We need to harvest the gardens and pack up everything now. We will not have much time to do so. If all four

~ 147 ~

of us work quickly, we can do this together in no time. It must be done now."

"You really feel we need to move after this?" I asked quietly.

Emy shook her head. "I am afraid it is so. Once I take Orthus, the town will not stop there. They might still go after more in fear. We cannot hide Samie forever. You can start fresh elsewhere, in safety."

I slumped in my chair. The inevitable was going to happen regardless of if I wanted it to or not.

So we headed out to the gardens to start our harvest. After some time, Tabitha appeared before me. We had all separated at this point in the day to get the harvest done quicker. I was alone in my work. Emy was nowhere near me; this would be the only reason why she would have dared to approach me at all. She thought she was safe.

"Hello, Sarah." She spoke with a tone of authority over me.

I rolled my eyes. "Good day, Tabitha. What else do you have to scorn about to me today?" I responded back as I wiped my hands on my apron. I didn't even bother to look at her.

"Well, first of all, you can rise up and address me with a little more respect." She tried to come off as though she held some high position or something.

"Oh please, Tabitha. What'd they do? Crown you Queen of all idiots or something?" I scoffed at her. "The only respect you will ever see from me will be that I am civil towards you when in fact you really deserve a beating for the way you have treated this family!"

She tried not to show that I had struck a nerve with my words. She kept her face stern and glanced away from me for a brief second. But, that was just enough time for me to see that I got under her skin right then.

"You are not to marry James, *ever*."

I laughed at her. "What are talking about? Who died and put you in charge of who I do and do not marry? I NEVER put you in charge of me and my love affairs. Be gone with you before I sic Emy on you!" I threatened her. She glanced around at Emy's name.

She stood just a little straighter. "You will not marry James because I am going to marry him."

"Oh like HELL you are!" I stood up from where I sat now. I could feel my blood boil within my veins now.

"Yes, yes I am!" she yelped back at me. She was clearly scared that I was on my feet so quickly.

"Over my dead body, Tabitha," I said through clenched teeth.

She smiled menacingly. "Those are just the words I wanted to hear from your lips." She pulled out a dagger from behind her and raised it over her head. "Now I can use this." She made to strike me with it. Suddenly, she was blinded by the sunlight.

The necklace! It is reflecting the sun into her eyes! I thought to myself. I punched Tabitha in the stomach and ran.

"Emy! Help!" I yelled as I ran. *'Damn it, Emy! Where are you?'*

Samie and Lor came running first. Emy was further away.

"What's wrong?" Lor asked.

"You witch! You used magic against me, you did! You made me fall!" Tabitha yelled from behind me.

Emy hitched up her skirts and ran faster to the scene.

"What are you claiming, Tabitha? Because from where I stand, you are the only one holding a dagger. Are you sure you were not pushed?" Emy glared at her.

"She made the sun blind me!" she screamed back.

"Do you mean the reflection off of the mirror around Sarah's neck?" Samie retorted back angrily.

"Well, well, well. And just who is this little lady, acting all big and bad?" Tabitha's eyes narrowed deeply on Samie. "Have not I seen you before? Perhaps in the village?"

Damn it, Samie! I thought to myself.

"You must be mistaken, Tabitha," I interjected. "She came with Lor. She has never been in town, ever."

'*Play along,*' I thought to Samie.

Samie nodded that she heard me. Tabitha tapped her finger along her chin. Then she waved her finger in the air. "No... I am certain I called her out as a witch. The villagers were trying to collect her for examination. In fact, Emy intervened in that whole scene. Why, however did you escape from that crowd, young lady? It had to have been by witch craft. You seemed to have just disappeared from the scene completely." Tabitha started to strut around us in a circle.

She nodded her head as she went. "I do believe that you are in fact Martha's daughter that Orthus has been looking for." She stopped right beside me and turned to Samie. "Isn't that correct, dear?" she asked Samie.

I pulled Samie behind me as she asked her. "Go away from here, Tabitha. You know nothing of what you are speaking of. I told you, she arrived here with Lor and the rest. She is an orphan James and I are going to adopt. So leave my child alone!" I warned her. "We TOLD you that you are mistaken, Tabitha. Why don't you leave from where you are not welcomed?"

"Isn't Orthus looking for his little PET by now?" Emy added sarcastically.

Tabitha looked slightly stricken by the remark. She stared us all down. "You are all liars. Each and every one of you. I know you are! I will prove that you are lying. You are liars, harlots, and witches! All of you! You will pay for this!" She hitched up her skirts and ran off from us.

"Remember, Tabitha!" I called out to her. "OVER MY DEAD BODY WILL YOU HAVE JAMES!"

Emy looked at me in shock and confusion. She shook her head at me in question.

I looked back at her, "She tried to tell me that she was going to have James for herself. I told her she was mistaken. She didn't let up so I said 'over my dead body'. Then she pulled out a dagger and came after me. That would be when I called for help and knocked her down as my necklace blinded her."

~ 151 ~

"What in the world is she thinking?" Emy shook her head in disapproval.

"I think she has gone mad," Lor piped in.

We all chuckled at that thought. We all agreed that we needed to get everything moving quicker after that little scene. We spoke very little the rest of the day. We decided none of us were safe alone after Tabitha tried to kill me. So we worked one area at a time together.

After some hours past, James and Aaron came home. James came running to me. "Are you hurt?" he asked me frantically.

I shook my head no. I was caught off guard by that question.

He squeezed me into a hug. "Thank goodness! I am glad that what I saw was not true!" he whispered.

I pulled away from him. "What do you mean?" I asked him, taking a step away from him. He seemed dumb founded by my question for a moment. He shook his head in thought.

"Were you in the gardens today?" he asked me seriously.

"Yes. We all were." I stared back at him puzzled by his question. *How does he know this?* I thought to myself.

"Did Tabitha show up for a visit?"

"Yes."

He put his hands upon my shoulders and very seriously asked me, "Did she have a dagger?"

"Yes," I whispered, staring into his eyes.

"What happened?"

"She tried to tell me that I wasn't going to marry you. I said over my dead body. She pulled out a dagger. She made to hurt me with it. But, my mirror caught the light and blinded her. I knocked her down and ran," I blurted out.

He looked relieved that I had gotten away.

"Now it's your turn. Fess up." I looked at him with my hands on my hips.

"Why, whatever do you mean?"

I took a step forward, hands still on my hips. "You know something, James. What do you know? What did you do?" I got nose to nose with him.

James threw his hands up in the air. "White flag!" He chuckled slightly to ease the tension that had now begun. "The necklace I got you is enchanted."

I looked at him with squinted eyes. "I'm waiting."

"I can explain. I had a protection put on it. Who so ever wears this," he lifted the mirror part up to play it over in his hands, "will be protected from any and all harm." He never looked up at me, just played with it more.

"How did you know it was Tabitha?" I whispered.

He slowly pulled his hands away and into his pocket. When they emerged again, there was a similar looking mirror in his hands. "It started to get warm."

I took the mirror from him.

"Then it flashed an image of Tabitha with a dagger going after you."

I placed my hands on his. "James, what did you do?" I asked him again. "Where did you get these?"

"I didn't believe that they would work like this! I swear it!" he blurted out. "I flashed it to the sky and prayed it not happen!"

I smiled. "James! It's alright! You unknowingly saved me! They are apparently connected to each other. When it sensed I was in danger, it flashed to you. You reacted and the sunlight you shined on it flashed through mine, thus blinding Tabitha long enough for me to get away!" I wrapped my arms around him and kissed him. "My hero," I whispered in his ear.

He returned my embrace. "I did, didn't I?" He sounded happier about it all now.

I stepped back. I pointed my finger at him. "This is our secret. No one is to know about this enchantment over these mirrors. Tabitha thinks I did something to have caused her to fall other than pushing her down. If she knew these actually helped to stop her..."

"She would lose her mind and cause us both to be gone."

I nodded. "Exactly. We must keep this quiet. Otherwise, our whole plan is done before we have started."

He nodded that he agreed.

"We should head inside and see if we can help with anything," I suggested.

After the meal, we laid our gatherings upon the table. Even Aaron and James helped for a time. After a time, there was a knock upon the door.

"I'll get it." Aaron stood up. "I need to stretch my legs anyways."

"Good evening, Father. How may we help you this evening?" Aaron's voice was faint at the door.

Emy glanced my way. I looked at James. I nodded and reassured him silently. *'Everything will be fine,'* I thought to him.

Father St. Paul stepped into the room, his hat in his hands.

"Tabitha was running her mouth in the village today. Something about witch craft and sorcery up here," he said softly.

"Of course she did," Emy spat out as she poured some coffee into a mug for the Father.

Father St. Paul raised his eyebrows. "Would you care to elaborate, child?"

"We were gathering herbs to be stored, and *Tabitha* appeared out of nowhere. She threatened Sarah. The sunlight reflected off of Sarah's new necklace and blinded her. Sarah was able to get away before Tabitha could harm her with the dagger she brought with her. Tabitha was angry that her pride got hurt by what did not go through for her, that she threatened all of us," Emy rattled off without skipping a beat.

Father St. Paul just sat there and listened quietly. When she was done, he thought a moment longer. "I see." We all sat there in silence, sorting our harvest. He started to sort as well. Some time passed before he spoke again. "I thought we were going to try and stay clear of Tabitha for now?"

"Like I said, she just showed up out of nowhere, demanding that Sarah not marry James," Emy replied.

"Tabitha did forget to mention <u>that</u> part." He nodded. "That seems more like her." He looked at me, "This is true, then?"

I nodded.

"What was your answer?"

"Over my dead body was she ever getting him. After she pressed me, that is," I replied.

It was his turn to nod. "I see. She planned this then. She wanted those words to come from your lips so she could react accordingly. She set you all up."

"It seems as though she is trying to get us all at once now. She is getting anxious about something," Emy said. "Otherwise just going after me should have been enough for her."

Father St. Paul nodded. "I did over hear her speaking with Orthus earlier. She seemed upset. It seems he promised her something of power and she wants payment now for it. She seems afraid that he might not follow through with the payment even if she does keep her end of the deal."

"She did make a deal with Orthus years ago," Emy informed the Father. "She has started to repay him now."

"A deal between the two of them? Let me guess, could it have something to do with the trials? She's already given him Martha. How many more does he need?"

"As many as he can get until he has me," Samie whispered

"And he promised your mother he will never touch you," Emy said.

"It's kind of early to be harvesting so much, is it not?" Father St. Paul quietly changed the topic.

"Yes it is. But I am afraid we must do this now instead of later. No one will be here to do anything later, I am afraid," Lor answered just as quietly.

"I see. When do you leave?"

There was a long silence at the table.

'Why don't you answer him, Emy?' I thought to her.

'But Aaron is here. He's not to know,' she shot back at me.

'Don't you think he's figured it out by now? He is not dumb. He's going to find out eventually. Would you rather he can say good-bye now or when it's too late?' I raised my brow at her.

She hung her head slightly and played with her fingers.

"When Tabitha has watched Emy burn at the stake," I blurted out finally.

"Emy?" Aaron whispered.

She never looked up. "Yes, this is true, Aaron. Tabitha has been working with Orthus. She will not rest until she has gotten me. But it will end with me."

"Why did you not say anything about this to me before? I could have helped," he whispered.

She stood up. "Helped with what, Aaron? There is nothing to help with. She will finally win with getting back at me. And I will stop Orthus at the same time. It will end with me."

"But—," Aaron started to rebut.

Emy cut him off. "It WILL END WITH ME," she roared.

He seemed to have shrunk with that. He thought about his words for a moment, lost in thought before opening his mouth again. "You always have to win, don't you?" he mustered.

Her heart sank with those words. "It's not about winning. It is about stopping someone who is undoubtedly so evil and making sure this does not continue is what it has always been about."

"It is just not fair." Aaron whispered and walked out of the room.

We all sat there in silence for a time, just sorting the table.

After some time, Aaron returned to the room. "I am going to get the ship ready to sail again very soon. I am heading into the village tonight to start getting things into order," he announced.

Emy stood up from the table and crossed the room. "Do not go because you are angry with me."

"I am not angry, just hurt that I cannot even help to protect my own wife. You never even gave me a chance to try," he responded.

"I am sorry that I cannot give you a chance to help. It really is out of my own hands at this point. There is nothing that anyone can really do."

"Then I am sorry as well. I will not stand around and watch as my wife willingly goes to the stake. I am going to set sail as soon as I can. You can either come with me or stay and die," he muttered.

"I choose to stay and die. This is my fate."

He breathed deeply and shook his head. "I was afraid of that." He kissed her forehead and went out the door. Emy just stood there, waiting.

James stood up. "I will speak with him tomorrow, if you would like?"

Emy never took her eyes off of the door. "You can try all you'd like. But, I do not feel that anything will get him to change his mind on this." She paused for a moment. "I think I shall go to bed now as it is getting late. Good evening, Father. Please do call again."

We let the Father out and made our ways to our resting areas as well. Tomorrow was another day.

In the morning, we were awakened to a heavy rapping upon the door. We all rushed to see who and what was going on. At the door were Tabitha, Nicolas, Orthus, and Father St. Paul.

"May we enter?" the Father asked solemnly.

"Well, now, I am very sorry, Father. My house is in a bit of disarray this morning. Perhaps we may go in the gardens? I will have Sarah bring us coffee." Emy gestured towards the gardens and away from the house.

'Do not let Orthus inside, AT ALL COSTS,' she threw into my head.

I nodded. "I shall be right out with the coffee."

They headed to the gardens and I started on the coffee.

"What could they possibly want at this hour?" James started to ask.

I shot him a look.

"Tabitha is getting her way," Samie said.

James put his head down. He sank in the seat by him. "Oh. That was stupid of me," he said.

"It wasn't all that dumb. It's early yet. We were caught off guard." I tried to comfort him. I started to get the water ready. Samie put some biscuits from the night before into a basket to bring out as well. When the coffee was ready, we gathered everything onto the tray and headed over to the gardens.

"Do you really believe that someone could cause a light to shine without a mirror to reflect it? You were pushed, Tabitha. Damn it, girl! Why do you always have to make everything so difficult for me? Why can't you learn? *When* will you learn to stop playing these games?" Emy demanded.

"It was sorcery, Emy. You know it, I know it. Stop fooling yourself," Tabitha shouted.

"You don't have a clue about what you are getting into, Tabitha. When will you stay out of things?" Emy stammered.

Tabitha went up close to Emy then walked behind Emy and leaned in next to her ear. "When I have Aaron, of course."

Emy grew red, including her energy, all around. Now the truth came out. The dragon had been provoked. Tabitha really did it this time. I stopped dead in my tracks, waiting what was to come next.

'Oh please do not let it be really happening. Please let it be an unreal vision! Something I can change!' I begged in my head.

'If you are seeing this, then I am, too,' Samie piped in.

Emy never moved her head. Only her eyes followed Tabitha around the other side of herself. "Well, well, well. So now the truth finally comes out. How long has this plan been in the works for? Have you just come to this plan on your own, now?"

Tabitha continued to circle around Emy, almost tauntingly. She smirked. "Oh, I have always wanted him. Ever since I can remember he and I are meant to be together. Not you and he. I think I made him see my way on that as of last night, too." She played her fingers along Emy's shoulders as she said it.

The fury built even greater within her with that thought. "What do you mean, Tabitha? What have you done to Aaron?" Emy started to go even redder now.

"Oh nothing much," Tabitha sang as she continued her little dance around Emy. "Why, someone had to comfort the poor soul at the shipyard last night. He was going on and on about how you said there was nothing he could do to help his poor little wifey poo from being... how was it? Ah, yes, burned at the stake by me?" She smiled sinisterly and stopped right in front of Emy.

I lost all feeling of my senses. My grip loosened on the tray. I stood there slightly out of my body and watched the tray crash upon the ground at my feet. My blood began to boil within my veins. *'How dare she!'* I spat in my thoughts to anyone who dared to listen. *'First James and now Aaron? The nerve of her! I shall kill her!'*

They all looked my way as the tray clambered upon the ground.

'Easy, Sarah. If you're not careful, even they will hear those thoughts,' Emy tried to soothe me.

I tried to regain control over my senses again. I swooped down to pick up the mess as quickly as I could. "I, I, I am terribly sorry! I must have tripped on a rock or something!" I lied.

"Samie, go get more coffee," I whispered as she knelt down beside me.

"Are you alright?" she whispered back at me.

"I shall be most fine as soon as I get my hands upon Tabitha!"

Samie's big brown eyes stared right into mine. "Do not do anything rash. I need you alive."

I thought on that one then nodded. "I promise."

Samie ran back to the cottage. I smoothed out my skirt and made my way back to the group. As I approached, Tabitha went all ear to ear grin. "Why here is the other harlot now!" She gleamed as though she was a child tattling on another to the grownups.

"What are you implying, Tabitha?" I glared at her.

"Why you know *exactly* what you and James have been up to! Come now! Do you *really* think we are all blind to the fact that you are under the same roof right now?" Her eyes glinted with that remark.

"What are you implying?" I demanded again.

"You are under the same roof. Harlot!" she screamed into my face.

"If I am a harlot like you are implying, then why does James have his own bedroom like he has for years?" I asked her softly.

I will kill you with kindness, wench. Just you watch, I thought silently.

"Oh come now. Do you really think anyone will believe that?"

"Why don't you go ask Aaron since you seem to think he's your 'pet' now?" I whispered back to her.

She seemed struck by that remark. She took a step back from me.

"Well, Father?" She turned on her heel to try and change the subject.

"Well what, child?" he asked as though he was day dreaming off in the corner.

"Are you going to charge them?" She stomped her foot in question to him.

"Charge who?" he asked as though he was a confused old man.

Well played, I thought.

"These two! Emy and Sarah!" she screamed. I could hear the tears starting on the back of her tone.

"Why? I see nothing wrong here except a grown woman throwing a temper tantrum because no one wants to play with her."

I had to stifle a giggle.

'Did he really just say that?' Emy poked at me.

'Pretty sure I heard that, too,' I poked back.

Tabitha's face went red. "What do you mean by those words, Father?" She clenched her fists as she spoke.

"Oh I am pretty certain you heard exactly what I said, Tabitha. Maybe Emy should be calling you the harlot since you are claiming to have gotten close to her husband Aaron last night?" He came closer to Tabitha.

She stared right into his eyes. After a few moments, Tabitha took a step back. "But I told you what Aaron revealed to me. Does that not count for *anything*?" Tabitha started to pout and whimper like a little child.

"What did he supposedly reveal to you that you didn't already know?" Emy spat.

Tabitha turned her head towards Emy. "You will not win this one. I have Aaron in my grasp now. He will be mine. You do not agree with each other. He told me about your plan. I know what you are up to this time! You will not have me tried!" Tabitha stammered.

I had to laugh out loud. Emy did, too.

"Do you seriously believe that I want you dead? What fun is there in death?" Emy glared at Tabitha.

'Watch what you say, Em,' I thought.

"Father! She said she would kill me when I was not expecting it! Does that not count for *something*?" she squealed now.

Father St. Paul sighed heavily. Orthus stepped next to him.

"Father, if you do not wish to have this put upon your shoulders, I can always take over this task instead for you. But, only if you really want me to. I do not mind bearing this heavy weight upon my shoulders."

I bet you don't, I thought silently.

Father St. Paul looked at Emy. She nodded to him. "Yes, I would very much rather that you took this case over. I cannot bear to condemn my own god-child."

"I am truly sorry to have had to put you through this. I never realized how close to this family you really were." Orthus put his hand on Father St. Paul shoulder in an act to comfort him, all while he smiled sinisterly at us.

Tabitha's face beamed bright. Orthus stood tall. Samie came up from behind me with new coffee.

"Emy, you have been accused of being a witch. I will need you to come with us into the village and stand trial," Orthus proclaimed.

I fell to the ground. I knew to expect this. I really did. But, when it actually happened, I was still not really ready for it after all. I lost all grip of my senses. I saw Samie run to Emy. James dropped down by my side. I felt his arms holding me. I never moved physically.

Tabitha went to Emy's face. "I TOLD you I would get you, darling. And it looks as though I get your husband to boot!"

Emy spat in her face.

Tabitha yelled. "Oh come now! Did you really think I would not play at that as well?" She chuckled as she wiped her face.

"You will be sorry for this, Tabitha. For *all* of this. Mark my words. You will rue this day!" Emy said in hushed tones with her head hung low.

Nicolas came up beside Emy. "This way, please," he said quietly while lightly guiding her arm towards their wagon.

Emy left silently with Nicolas. Tabitha came towards me. James wrapped his arms tighter around me. "You will be next, Sarah. Just you wait. I will get you as well. Then, Samie will be *all* mine," she cooed as she smirked over her little win of the day.

I slipped back within myself. My head moved up slowly towards Tabitha. I glared at her. I rose so slowly to meet her level. My eyes never left hers. Her smirk disappeared as I rose. "You will never get to *my* child. You cannot *kill* me. You will *never* kill me. You will be sorry for this day. You will be sorry that that you ever started this whole fiasco." I stared at her through my fallen hair.

Now she looked completely scared by my words.

'No one. Not even your precious Orthus will be able to stop me from getting to you. You are done here,' I thought at her.

She ran over to Orthus. She kept looking behind her as the made their way to the wagon as well. I never took my eyes off of Tabitha.

"I do so hope Emy was right in this plan of hers," Father St. Paul whispered.

"I hope so, too, Father. I hope so, too. You best be going before they suspect you as well."

He tilted his hat and took off as well. Samie came towards us. "Go tell Lor to get the men to pack everything into a wagon, now."

"Are we not staying to help?" she asked, confused.

I turned to her. "I need everything ready now. We will do what we must. But, from afar. We cannot risk anymore."

She nodded and ran off to find Lor.

"Are you sure of this?" James turned me towards him.

"Positive." We then headed to the cottage to start sorting everything.

Later that night, Nicolas was at the door.

"What news?" I asked.

Nicolas removed his hat. "May I come in?"

I opened the door to allow him in.

"The trial is set for tomorrow." He frowned.

"They are surely not wasting any time on Emy," James scoffed.

"Of course not. Tabitha is scared out of her mind right now. The sooner Emy is gone, the sooner she *thinks* she can get to me next," I shot bitterly.

Lor laughed. "Won't she be surprised when she finds that we have left without a trace!"

I had to chuckle at that thought. "Yes, we will be pulling one upon her, won't we?"

We all had a good laugh at that thought. Nicolas fretted with his fingers. He seemed nervous in his thoughts.

"What is the matter?" Samie asked.

Nicolas jumped as though he was startled by the question.

"What is on your mind, Nicolas?" Samie rephrased her question.

"Well, I was just wondering…" He trailed off.

We all looked at him, waiting for him to finish his thought.

"Wondering what?" I coaxed.

"Can I come, too?" he asked sheepishly.

James looked at me. He shrugged. *'That is up to you, love,'* he thought to me.

"Why do you want to come with the ones who will be doing away with Orthus?" I asked him.

"Because there will be nothing left here for me. That and I do not want to stay with my cousins. They are just as bad as Orthus is. I cannot keep living like this anymore. I have chosen my side. I hope you will accept me as well."

I smiled. "That is the best answer I could have ever hoped for! You may come with us. Start sneaking your belongings out."

Samie jumped up from her seat and hugged Nicolas. "I am so happy that you can come!" She squealed with delight. I do believe I saw Nicolas blush at this.

"I can bring most of my things tomorrow during the trial. No one will be home to see me. No one will miss me at the trial either."

"Then it is decided. We will see how tomorrow progresses. Aaron is not to know about any of this from here on in. The last thing we need is for him to interfere with us fleeing to safety after everything takes place."

We spent the rest of the evening going through everything to see what could stay.

The next day at the trial, the whole village converged inside the meeting hall. James, Samie, and I tried to go towards the side of the building. We really did not want to be seen. I was afraid that things might get out of hand with this one.

"Order! Order!" the judge called out, banging his gavel.

Slowly, the room hushed.

"Bring in the prisoner." He motioned to Nicolas.

Nicolas nodded and left the room. He came back slowly with Emy next to him. He showed her to the seat for the accused. She decided to remain standing.

"You may have a seat, Miss Emy," the judge offered.

"No, thank you, your Honor. I shall like to stand so that I may have a good look at all of the good folk of this village that shall be accusing me," she responded coldly.

"Very well, then. Shall we begin?"

Orthus came out of nowhere. He started to pace back and forth in front of everyone. "Emy has been accused of being a witch by not only her cousin Tabitha, but now also by her own husband, Aaron!"

The group murmured.

"When will this stop in our village? When will the witches cease to be?" he asked more forcefully.

Cheers from the group now. Someone yelled, "Burn the witch!"

Someone else yelled, "She cursed my farm!"

I turned my eyes towards that voice. *'Liar. We never even set foot near your farm!'* I thought, enraged.

Then, I saw Jared standing behind her, whispering in her ear.

"My child became ill!" another spoke out.

This time, his cousin, and Nicolas' twin, Mathais was whispering in his ear.

"How *dare* they!" I whispered under my breath.

"What is it?" James whispered back.

"Mathais and Jared are in on this scheme."

"How so?" James asked, struggling to be heard above the shouts.

"They are standing behind the ones doing the outbursts and *making* them say these things! *None* of it is true! We've never set *foot* on their farm! His kid was sick before they came into the village!" I explained.

"This is an outrage!" Samie piped in. "I don't believe them!"

"Should we try and stop them?" James suggested.

"And cause all of us to be part of this fiasco? Hell, no. Just leave it all as it is. We are safer to just let them have their 'fun'," I stammered.

The gavel banged loudly, echoing throughout the hall. "Order!" the judge yelled.

The room hushed quickly.

"Does she carry the mark?" someone shouted from the crowd.

Orthus smiled. He gestured to one of the older women from the church. She stood up and came forward.

"Did you find a mark on the woman in question?" Orthus asked her softly.

She nodded, hesitantly.

"*Where* did you find the mark?" Orthus asked just as softly.

The woman looked at Emy, then around the room. She closed her eyes. "On her back, there was a marking." She bent her head low.

'The scar that we could never explain where it came from,' I thought. *'Of course they would use that.'*

James looked at me. "What mark does she have on her back?" he asked me, puzzled.

"It's near her shoulders. We don't know whence it came from. It has always been there for as long as we can remember."

"Then she is found guilty of being a witch! If she carries the mark, then she must be!" the judge ruled.

The entire room flooded with murmurs and chatter. I glanced at Emy. Our eyes met.

'It will be fine. All is how it must be,' she pressed into my thoughts.

I nodded back to her.

"Let us be gone from here. I cannot stand to stay in this room any longer with these people," I said out loud to no one in particular.

Samie and James followed me out. As we headed to the wagon, there was a voice from behind me.

"Well, well, well. It looks as though I have won yet again. Just when will you all learn that I deserve everything? Just give me what I want, and I will spare you of this same fate," Tabitha said gleefully.

Oh, how I wish I could punch you right in the face right now, I thought silently. I smiled back at her and said, "Isn't two cousins and a stranger enough for you? I'd thought that Orthus would have surely tired of you by now" I turned back towards the wagon.

"If you are not careful, I just might have to have them start looking at you next." Tabitha snickered at me.

"If one is not careful, herself, she may just find herself on the receiving end of her own game. Now leave us be, Tabitha!" I sneered back at her. My blood was starting to boil within my veins. I climbed into the wagon and nodded for James to start going.

"You have not heard the last of this, Sarah!" she yelled at us. The villagers started to crowd around her to see what the commotion was that she was creating.

'Oh yes I have, Tabitha. It ends now,' I pressed into her head. I heard nothing in response from her after that.

When we arrived back to the cottage, Nicolas was waiting outside with Lor. His wagon was all packed up and ready to go. They stood when they saw us approaching. Once we were all out of the wagon, Lor asked, "How did it turn out?"

"She was found guilty without any doubt. Jared and Mathais were there to ensure that she was found guilty, too. The sneaks were whispering in others ears and telling them what to say."

"Why does it not surprise me that those two would be there egging things like that on?" Nicolas blurted. He shook his head. "I am truly sorry that they did that to Emy. They have always been cruel like that. Even to me."

"I am sorry that your own twin would do such a thing considering how you felt for Cloe. Surely he knew your feelings for her?" I placed his hands in mine to console him. "Fear not, we will be leaving even them behind us. They will torment you no longer." Nicolas smiled wan smile in response.

"Now let us be going. We will not have long to pack up whatever else we can before they follow through with the rest," I reminded them.

We spent the rest of the day organizing as much as possible into the wagons. We kept enough for the main quarters to look as though we still lived there to throw off anyone else.

While getting the table ready for dinner, I placed an extra setting. James and Samie looked at me questioningly. The broom fell over in the corner.

"Company's coming," Lor said aloud.

Suddenly, there was a knock upon the door.

"How did you know?" Samie started to ask.

James went to answer the door.

Father St. Paul entered into the kitchen. I gestured the open seat to him. "Please."

We all sat and ate our meal in silence. Only after all was done did I finally speak. "How is she?"

"She is well. Handling it all very nicely. I have made sure her and Martha get some extra food," Father St. Paul answered.

"Any word on when they will finish this?" I pressed in.

"Another day or two from what I am hearing. Tabitha seems to want this done as soon as possible," he informed us.

"Of course she does...because she thinks that she will be able to touch me after Emy is gone," I said.

He tilted his head. "She can't now?"

"Oh no. As long as Emy was aware of Tabitha going after me, she was always shielding me. I think that she feels when Emy goes, so goes her shield. What she lacks is the fact that I have been protecting myself from her for years on my own now. Emy only increases mine." I smiled sweetly.

"Won't she be surprised when she still cannot touch you." He chuckled.

I laughed with him.

"Will you be there on that day?" he asked, serious now.

I shook my head. "Not where anyone will see us, no. We will be carefully watching from afar. Just to make sure all goes as planned."

He nodded. "Sounds like a safer plan. This way Tabitha cannot try to point any fingers on any of you during all of this."

He stood up and tilted his head to me. "Good evening to all of you. Thank you for the lovely meal. I shall be back as soon as I find any more information to be found."

James escorted him to the door.

Again Samie pressed me. "How did you know he was coming over?"

"I just knew." I shrugged.

Then she looked at Lor. "Why did you say company was coming when the broom fell?"

"Because if a broom falls for no apparent reason, that is just what it means. That company is coming."

Samie nodded that she understood.

"I am tired. I think I shall retire to bed now. We have a long two day trip ahead of us." I stood up. James walked me to the stairs.

"I am going to make sure the grounds are secure," he said.

I nodded. "That sounds good. I do not feel any of them will be by tonight, but it is better to be safe than sorry." I gave him a kiss on his forehead and headed up the stairs.

In the morning, Father St. Paul was back.

"They will be doing Martha today and Emy tomorrow," he informed us.

"So close together? Samie asked.

The Father nodded. "Yes, they want to hurry before they try to do anything together. They are becoming afraid now."

"That is not a good sign. They will start looking at anyone they can now," James said sadly.

 Which is exactly why we will not be at either one of them while it is happening," I said.

"But–," Samie started to protest.

I put my hand up to silence her. "Not right now."

Samie slouched into the only seat left in the room.

'We will hide in the trees to watch and remove her once all have left to bury her in private,' I thought to her.

She looked up at me, puzzled.

I turned to Father St. Paul. "Thank you so much for all of your help with all of this, Father. You have eased my mind on many things."

He took my hands. "It was nothing, my child. I am only glad that I could be helpful. Will you be in the same place, later?" he asked softly.

I nodded.

"Then I will make sure there is a wagon nearby so I can help you bury Martha later," he informed me.

"Will you not get into trouble for helping us?" I asked, puzzled.

"Things have already gone array around here, I feel that I can try to redeem even a little tiny bit with these small acts," he explained his feelings to me.

"I see." I smiled. "Rest assured no good deed goes unnoticed. It makes a huge difference to us here, if that is of any consolation. We greatly appreciate all that you have ever done or shown to our family. I am truly sorry that things have turned out the way that they have and I hope we may all be able to overcome this tragedy."

He turned to Samie. "Samie, dear, I know that you and your mother may not have started off with this family. That you are not even blood. But this family has welcomed you with opened and loving arms. I can only pray that you know just how truly blessed you are to still have a family to call yours after this is all over."

Samie bowed to him. "Yes, Father, I do know that I have been truly blessed at this second family," she whispered.

"You as well, Nicolas. Your own family is ridden with evil traits. And yet, you still prevail to be good. You are willing to abandon your true family and enter into a better and happier household so you are no longer tempted with their evil deeds. In that, I applaud you in your ongoing task to remain good. I pray that you have found your true home now," he said to Nicolas.

"Thank you, Father. It gives me strength to know that you feel I am going down the right path. I am glad that I have your blessing in this," Nicolas answered the Father.

"You do, you all do. I pray that after all of this I will see you all again." He did not say anything more on that topic.

'Does he know our plan?' Lor interjected into my head.

'It seems so. Now is not the time to ask what can be kept secret a while longer,' I thought back to her.

"I should be going. There will be lots to do today and tomorrow I am afraid." The Father put his hat back on and made for the door.

"Thank you again, Father, for all the news." James saw him out.

"It is good to know he is on our side through this," Lor said after James returned to the room.

"Yes, it is truly a comfort in that," I agreed.

"What did you mean by we will but we won't be there?" Samie pressed now. She did not want to wait any longer.

I looked at Lor, then at Samie. "There is a clearing hidden amongst the trees. We can hide there and watch everything in protection. We cannot afford Tabitha to see any of us today. Otherwise, the entire plan is ruined."

"It is of great importance that we stay within the cover of these particular trees. They will be our only protection while we watch this."

"Why? What is so special about this clearing?" Samie narrowed her eyes at us.

James looked puzzled. "Is this the same clearing when we were kids?" he asked us.

I nodded. It was both of our mother's favorite spot. They would bring us down from time to time. They would practice different things with in the trees. We were always told never to leave it unless one of them was with us. We were safe as long as we stayed with in it.

"Our mothers' put a protection spell on it years ago, before we were born. They needed a place they could go and be safe. But they were afraid for us as well," I explained.

"To keep us safe? From what?" James started.

I turned to Nicolas. "Was your family here when we were all little?"

Nicolas thought a moment. "I believe so."

I nodded and looked at James. I raised my eye-brows. "Sounds like they knew about Orthus before we did. Do you not think so? Why else would they have needed to go into a secret spot and keep us protected at the same time?"

"Possibly, but since neither one are here to be asked anymore, we shall never know." James said quietly.

We were silent for a time, lost in our own thoughts. After some time, I said, "Let us be going now. Things should be starting soon, I would think."

They all nodded and we started out the door.

"Should we take the wagon?" James asked.

"No. Father St. Paul will have one waiting for us later. Besides, if someone sees the wagon but we are nowhere to be seen, there will be suspicions. We are safer walking," I explained.

They all nodded.

"Sarah's right. The big wagon is hard to hide. We can hide behind trees in secret," Lor said.

We walked out of the house in silence.

When we got to the clearing, the platform was still being stacked. The villagers were still slowly coming out to the area. Samie started to go to the edge of the clearing.

"Remember to stay within the trees. We are safest with in the ring." James said softly to Samie. He rested a hand on her shoulder.

"I will," she responded.

We just sat there quietly on the rocks scattered throughout the clearing and waited until it was time.

Finally, we heard louder murmurs going on. Lor and I stood up. We nodded to each other. It was time to begin. We all stepped closer to the edge of the clearing. They started to bring Martha over.

Orthus looked distressed this time. There was sadness behind his eyes. He closed his eyes and breathed deeply. It seemed as though he was holding his breath.

Finally, he began to speak. "Martha! You have been found guilty of being a witch and have been sentenced to death by burning. Do you have any last words before you go?"

She stood straight and tall. "I only pray and hope that my last request I have made will be followed through after I am gone. That person knows of the request and I shall not subject them to humility that they would so deserve for I am not of that nature of a person. I pray that God will watch over the village I have come to love as home and family for years to come." She remained looking straight ahead.

"Do you have anything more to add?" Orthus whispered to her.

"No, I am through here," she said sternly.

He looked as though he was slapped across the face with that answer. "Very well," He replied. He nodded and stepped away.

They bound her to the pole and came with the torches. She never moved. She never even screamed when the flames licked at her feet.

Samie fell to the ground, crying. "Mama," she whispered among her tears.

I stood and watched Orthus waiting beside the flames. He looked sad.

'You don't have to do this, you know. There is always room for change,' I thought to him.

'It is too late for me. Nicolas has a chance, though. Take him with you. Guide him,' he thought back.

'Take him where?' I pressed.

'Anywhere but here with me; away from his brother and cousin. They are too far gone as well. We are all past the point of no return.' He shook his head.

Martha's body was engulfed in the flames now. Her spirit willingly rose above her. She looked over at Orthus and held out her arms to him.

'Is she willingly giving herself to him?' I thought to Lor.

'It appears so,' Lor thought back.

I shook my head.

"What is he up to now?" James blurted out suddenly.

Lor, Samie, and I all turned. Orthus was stepping away. He turned his back to Martha's spirit. Was he not going to take her? Did he really love her so much that he would not dare to take her essence? Martha's spirit blew him a kiss and disappeared from sight. Orthus had a small smile on his face when she left.

"Good-bye, Mama," Samie whispered.

We all bowed our heads in silence. Time passed and slowly the villagers left the burning site. Smoke still came from the mound around Martha's body. Father St. Paul came over with a wagon. He pulled out clothes to wrap Martha's body up in. We stepped out from our hiding place. No one said a word. We just worked together to gather Martha for burial. We placed her on the large cloth and carefully wrapped her burnt body. We placed her in the bed of the wagon and climbed in as well. Nicolas took the reins. The only sound through the dark night was the clomp of the horses hooves along the ground and the creaking of the wagon wheels. Even the animals were silent. Father St. Paul found the willow tree where we had buried Cloe earlier in the year.

"I think she will like it here," Samie said solemnly.

I nodded. "Yes, it is our favorite quiet spot as well. A lovely resting place for her to rest."

We laid her to rest in the ground near Cloe and her wolf. We stood beside her grave in silence as Father St. Paul said a few words. I patted Samie's back after some time. We all walked back to the wagon to give Samie some time alone with her mother.

"What time is Emy's?" I asked Father St. Paul when I felt we were far enough away.

"Towards night fall," Father St. Paul replied.

"You will see to all of her final arrangements?"

He nodded. "Yes, I have a few brothers here visiting to help me. They have taken the vow of silence so I know they can be trusted. We grew up together in the monastery."

I nodded.

"I plan to leave with them when they leave. I cannot stay here after all that has transpired," he continued.

"I understand," I whispered.

"Maybe I shall travel, like Lor does. You know, from village to village. I can offer help if they need it wherever I go."

I smiled. "That sounds like a wonderful idea for you. Maybe you will come across some old friends along the way."

He smiled in return. "I hope so. I think if I did, I may remain there for a time."

"That would be nice. To stay if you found friends you have missed, that is," I agreed.

Samie came walking back to where we all waited for her. "I'm ready now," she said, drifting.

We all got back into the wagon and proceeded back home.

"Goodnight, Father," I said as we climbed out of the wagon once we arrived at the cabin.

~ 185 ~

He tilted his hat. "Good-bye until we meet again." He winked.

I smiled. "Good-bye until we meet again, then."

I watched him ride off to the village to prepare for tomorrow.

"Did you tell him our plan?" James asked from behind me.

I shook my head. "No, he just knows stuff. It is how he is. He understands without ever having to be told."

"Then we are still safe to do so secretly?" he asked.

I turned towards him. "Of course we are. Let us be going now. I want to be sure we have all that we need."

We worked through the night to ensure all was in order.

Come the morning, we tended the gardens one last time and gathered any livestock that had survived Orthus' spat earlier on.

"I think that shall do it," Lor said as she wiped her hands.

"I hope so. Now it will still look as though we are still here for a time, to throw them off?" I made sure with Lor.

She nodded. "Yes, do not fret. All is set. They will never be the wiser to the fact that we have left."

She placed her hands on my shoulders. "They will think we never left," she whispered.

"Good." I sighed. We closed the door to the cottage one last time. The wagons moved to the hillside that led near the village.

Most of the wagons went up ahead. A few of us remained at the larger hill.

"What is wrong?" Nicolas asked.

I waved my hand up. "Nothing is the matter. I want to watch something," I answered. I jumped down from the wagon.

"You're not going to watch Emy are you?" Nicolas asked, jumping down behind me.

I turned on my heel. "I said I am going to watch something. She is my sister. I'm not going to leave her alone in this. We are safe enough away. No one will know we are here and where we have gone to. Just wait here," I stammered.

Nicolas backed away, raising his hands like a white flag. "Alright, alright. Do what you must."

I heaved a sigh of relief. "Thank you." I turned back to where I was walking. I reached the edge of the trees. I could see the area ready for Emy. They built a landing nearby it. Tabitha was waiting next to Orthus. She looked as though she was holding back a smile. She tried hard to keep her face stern and serious.

'Oh what a tangled web you have woven yourself and this family into,' I thought at her.

She looked around. *'Where are you at, dear cousin?'*

I shook my head. *'Wouldn't you just love to know that one? Alas, that is my secret, where I hide. You shall never touch me. That was vowed long ago. But, you shall never touch Samie, either. Like Emy dies today to protect me, I shall die to protect Samie. Today is the end of this, Tabitha. There will be no more.'*

~ 187 ~

I saw her laugh slightly. *'I know where you live. Do not underestimate me. I shall have you both.'*

'Go ahead.' I smirked. *'But I think that it is you who underestimates me. You will be quite surprised when you get there. I assure you.'*

'What do you mean by that?' I could see in her face she was getting angry.

'Oh, dear, and ruin the surprise I have for you? You will just have to wait and see.' I toyed with her.

'Fine.' She stood straighter. *'I shall wait then.'*

Everyone was assembled now. They led Emy closer to the landing. Aaron was standing next to Tabitha now. Emy kept her head held high and proud. She knew what she was doing, even if the villagers were unaware of the real situation.

They threw stuff at her and yelled things to her. She never said a word. She never even flinched. She stepped onto the landing and all fell silent. They watched her closely. Emy leaned close to Aaron's ear and whispered something there.

Aaron stood still and turned pale white. His jaw dropped to the ground.

'What did you say to him?' I thought out to Emy.

'Never mind that, shouldn't you be gone from here?' she snapped back at me.

'I am far enough away. All is set and in place,' I retorted.

She shook her head. She came to Tabitha next. She looked her up and down. Tabitha refused to look directly at her. I could see her shake as Emy came closer. Emy leaned into Tabitha and kissed her cheek. She whispered in her ear as well. Disdain and anger appeared on Tabitha's face as Emy walked away.

'Can I at least know that one?' I smirked.

'I told her I'd see her in hell.' She chuckled.

I laughed out loud. *'I love you dearest sister.'* I held back my tears. *'I know this is meant to go this way. I accept that. I don't like it. But I understand.'*

'Love you as well. Keep all safe. I will always be near,' she answered.

They guided her to the pole and tied her hands behind it. She looked straight ahead.

Orthus began his spiel. "Emy, you have been found guilty of being a witch. You are condemned to burn in fire in hopes of saving your soul. Do you have any last words to share?"

Emy never moved. "No, no I have nothing to say."

"Very well then." Orthus nodded. Two men came from either side with torches. They touched them to the logs under Emy's feet. Soon the fire crackled and rose. They licked at Emy's feet. Emy closed her eyes. Her lips whispered among the crackling flames. Father St. Paul was in the shadows saying his own prayers.

Soon, Emy's spirit rose from her body. Orthus tried to take her. She turned towards him. She stared at him. He tried again. Nothing. He was powerless against whatever spell she did.

'I am not fully dead yet, Orthus.' I heard her in my head speaking to him.

He looked at her, confused. "How can this be?" he whispered.

Tabitha looked at him. 'What are you doing?' she thought out to all of us.

"How are you not dead yet?" he stammered to Emy's spirit.

'Oh, I have a few tricks up my sleeve, dearie. You and Tabitha have underestimated me severely. Your power drains as you use it. The more you attack me, the more I am absorbing your energy. You cannot touch me, Emy thought back.

"I don't believe you." Orthus glared at her spirit. To anyone else, there was nothing there. He tried harder this time to attack her spirit.

Her spirit laughed heartily. She glowed brighter. 'It is useless to keep trying.' She raised her hand towards him. A ray of light shot at him. He fell where he stood. He stood up and tried again. Again, it was of no use. Emy only absorbed more.

'You feeble minded man. I almost feel sorry for you. When will you learn?' she asked him solemnly.

'I don't have to learn nothing. It is you who must learn.' He turned to the men with the torches from earlier. "More logs! The witch fights her death!"

Emy shot one last long blast of energy at him. He fell back again, this time knocking Tabitha over. Tabitha rolled him off of her. Emy went back to her body. Another small light came up from her body. I stared hard. The light went into her arms and seemed to snuggle there.

Could it be?

'Father, make sure you put mother and child on the marker, please.' I thought to him.

'Not to worry, it shall be done,' he thought back to me.

I watched Emy and her unborn child disappear to the beyond. Orthus did not move from where Tabitha had rolled him off of her. I turned to the wagon. "Time to be going from this cursed place," I announced.

We all climbed back into the wagons and disappeared ourselves into the darkness, hopefully forever.

*   *   *

Many years later.

I am just kneeling in the gardens, weeding what needs to be. It was a quiet, peaceful morning. Everyone else was off doing their own thing by this time of day. A shadow stood over me.

"Hello, Sarah. Tis good to see you again," a familiar voice said.

I lifted my head up, trying to see under my hat. The face was a lot older than I had remembered. Could it really be? "Father St. Paul?" I asked.

He smiled bright. That smile I remembered. He opened his arms for a hug. "Yes, Sarah. See, I told you it was good-bye until we met again."

I got up and gave my dear friend a hug. "It is good to see you again. Please, come up to the cottage. Can you stay a while?" I asked.

He nodded. "As long as I like."

We walked up to the cottage in the bright sunlight with hope for the future.

Made in the USA
Middletown, DE
10 May 2022

65372440R00109